The summer sun was intensely hot, the wind light and erratic. As she slid off into the water after Jane, Deb recalled her relief when Amy left too preoccupied that morning to ask what Deb would be doing that day. She felt Jane brush against her, and she swam a little away from the boat.

"Let's put in for lunch," Jane suggested, pushing the craft toward shore.

The barn, shafted with sunlight beaming through broken boards, was cool and deserted. Old hay and straw littered the floor and dust motes danced in the hazy shafts of light. Jane placed the towel carelessly on the straw, then looked directly into Deb's eyes.

A stab of excitement electrified Deb. She ran her tongue nervously over her lips and watched Jane's slow, knowing smile.

"I can't do this," Deb said, recognizing it as a lie.

Jane said, "You wouldn't be here today if you didn't want to."

The Naiad Press, Inc.
1991

Printed in the United States of America on acid-free paper
First Edition

Edited by Katherine V. Forrest
Cover design by Pat Tong and Bonnie Liss
(Phoenix Graphics)
Typeset by Sandi Stancil

Library of Congress Cataloging-in-Publication Data

Calhoun, Jackie.
Second Chance / by Jackie Calhoun
p. cm.
ISBN 0-941483-93-2 : $9.95
I. Title.
PS3563.A3985S43 1991
813'.54--dc20 91-22266
CIP

About the Author

Jackie Calhoun (author of *Lifestyles*) was born and grew up in Wisconsin, lived in Indiana for twenty-seven years, and moved back to Wisconsin in 1987. She divides her time between her home and cottage. This is her second novel.

To Chris, for loving support.

To my daughters, Janny and Jessica, for acceptance.

To David, for insight.

Although certain geographical locations are actual, the characters and story in this novel are fictitious.

I

Soft breathing bathed Amy's neck with little puffs of warm air. She turned her head toward the window, a gray outline in the coming dawn. Outside a cardinal sang repetitively. She smiled. The blinds stirred and rattled a little, letting in more light as a spring breeze blew them inward. She put a leg and arm on top of the sheet, and the woman next to her sighed and moved closer. Amy glanced at the disheveled dark head resting against her shoulder, at black curling lashes closed against soft curve of cheek.

She ran a tentative finger over the smooth skin, down the cheek and neck to collar bone and shoulder, and felt the other woman's body awaken and stretch against her own. Startling green eyes looked into hers. Amy cleared her throat. "Morning, Deb," she said, her own voice husky from sleep.

"Morning." Deb's mouth widened in a crooked smile. "Sleep well?"

"Mmmm," Amy replied, "and you?"

"Very." She stretched again and her lips, soft and searching, closed over Amy's.

Amy responded at first, then reluctantly pulled herself away and rolled her legs over the side of the bed. "We don't have time," she said.

"You're right, we don't," Deb agreed.

Amy felt regret, a constriction of stomach muscles. Gritting her teeth she padded into the bathroom, Deb on her heels. Amy stepped under the shower and watched as Deb climbed in after her. They took turns under the stream of water as if they had been showering together for years — Deb shaving while Amy washed her hair, then changing places.

They ate breakfast and watched the early morning news, then held each other close before leaving the apartment to go their separate ways. Amy beeped and waved as Deb raised a hand through the sunroof of her Subaru, turning it south off Ridge Road. Amy pointed her Grand Am north and watched the Subaru in her rearview mirror until it was swallowed up by other vehicles and distance.

It was time to devote her attention to the rental business she owned and managed. Forgetting everything but the uncertainty of her future, she clenched her teeth. Certain bills had to be paid before the doors opened today. Somehow she'd have to juggle funds. Without recall of the drive there, she parked behind the rental store and entered the cool, musty-smelling building where she walked past rototillers, aerators, thatchers and mowers, to her office. It was spring despite the wet cool weather which only slowed down the rush to tend lawns and gardens.

At seven-thirty Ted poked his head in the door of her office. "Just wanted you to know I was here, boss lady."

She glanced up and smiled at his bulky frame. "What's going out this morning?"

"Haven't checked yet, but I know I have to deliver a backhoe. John comin' in?"

"I don't know, I doubt it." John hadn't shown much interest in the business since she had left him. She shrugged and ran a hand over her face. "We need more help. See if Leonard can come to work, will you?" It meant a larger payroll, an endless circle of money chasing money, always running away from her. She watched Ted's retreating back, heard him lift the phone at the counter. Then the other line rang and she picked it up.

"Netzger Rentals."

"Do you have something to get wallpaper off walls?"

"Sure do. We have wallpaper steamers." Actually, they had two wallpaper steamers.

"Great. Rolly's Rent All is all out. Can you hold one for me?"

Amy winced at the mention of Rolly's Rent All, the major competition on the north side of the city.

Rolly's seemed to have unlimited money and inventory. She buzzed the counter and told Ted to put a hold on a wallpaper steamer.

"I got to get that backhoe loaded and get out of here," Ted answered. "I'm the only one at the counter."

Meaning she had to take his place. She closed the office door and carried the mail to the counter. The two phone lines lit up as Ted headed out the side door. "Hurry back," she called, "and get the money in advance. When's Leonard coming in?"

"Thirty minutes," Ted replied, holding the door open and spitting onto the parking lot.

Thirty minutes could be like thirty hours in this business, she reflected, and as if to reinforce the thought, two customers came in. After giving rates to those on the phone, she took the receiver off the hook, punched the other line on, and spoke to the first customer, an older, grim-faced man.

"I need to make a garden. You got someone I can talk to about it."

He wanted a man to discuss gardening with, she knew. She bridled and then pulled her anger up short. With Rolly's right around the corner she couldn't afford an annoyed customer. "Maybe I can help you. How big a garden do you want?"

"Big, the whole back yard."

"You might need a tractor and plow then."

"The yard's fenced, walk-through gate," he grunted.

"Oh well, that lets out a tractor." She pointed at the row of rototillers. "That's the next best thing, a tiller with rear tines."

"How'm I gonna get that home?"

"Well, we can drive it in a truck or trailer. Have you got a hitch?"

"Then you get my money for a truck or a trailer or a hitch. I know how that goes. Ends up costing a bundle."

Amy shut her mouth and shrugged. Let him decide. She glanced at the other customer, a younger man who was leaning against the counter listening to their conversation. "You want to think about it then?" she asked.

"What do you think?" The older man turned to the younger one.

"It's hard to till sod," the other man said knowingly.

Amy knew that but there was no other option. Another day dealing with chauvinists, she thought. She had spent the past fifteen years struggling to be treated as an equal in this male-oriented business. She knew more about the equipment she rented and what it could do than most men, including Ted who had learned what he knew about the rental business from her. But to try to convince some man off the street of that was like pounding her dog's head because the animal couldn't talk.

She felt the thud against her leg and automatically reached down to pat the dog. No wonder the analogy had occurred to her. It meant John was in the store or on the grounds somewhere. "How are you, Grit?"

Grit panted in reply, his yellow brown eyes adoring her, his tail now beating against the back of the counter.

"Phew, you smell, Grit."

The dog's tail drooped, he licked his lips nervously.

"But it's okay, dogs are supposed to smell." Her voice conveyed approval. The tail rose and thudded harder.

"Nice dog," the younger man said, looking over the counter at Grit.

"Thanks," she said. Then to the older man, "Look, John Netzger's here someplace. Would you like to talk garden with him? I'll find him."

"Looking for me?" John threaded his way through the generators.

"Yeah," Amy said, "this man wants to turn his back yard into a garden. He wants to know the best way to do it."

"You can tell him that, Amy." John sipped coffee out of a styrofoam cup.

"Well, he'd rather talk to a man." She turned to the younger man, who was exhibiting signs of restlessness. "Sorry about the delay. Can I help you?"

"I want to rent a thatcher, get all that dead grass out of my lawn."

Amy glanced outside at the puddles standing in the parking lot and shook her head. "I'd love to rent you one, but it's really too wet out to do the job. It'll bog down; the knives'll pick up mud, but if you still want one, it's yours."

The man looked annoyed. Sometimes people didn't want their plans sidetracked. "I set aside today to thatch the yard."

Amy slapped a contract on the counter and

smiled. She could hear John repeating her advice, patiently expounding on the best way to make land ready for garden. It annoyed her; they all annoyed her. She ran a palm over Grit's head. One of the dog's haunches pressed into her foot. She felt his tongue warm on her hand.

After the contract was filled out, she helped the man lift the thatcher and fit it in his trunk. Then she returned to the counter and hung up the phone. John was showing the older man the rear-mounted tillers. "Sure, I'll be glad to take care of it," she heard him say, as the other man left the store.

"What the hell? All that and he's not going to rent anything?"

"I told him I'll take it to him and help him."

Amy shook her head. "John, that's no way to do business."

"He'll pay the rental."

"And your time?" She raised her eyebrows.

"That was Harley Daniels. He's one of the old boys from around here."

"I see. You've known him all your life, right?"

"Yep, and he's got all his insurance with me."

"John, I think I want to sell," she said abruptly.

He threw the styrofoam cup at the wastebasket and missed. She leaned down and put it in. "What'll you do?" he grunted.

"I could work in the insurance business. I'm tired of this hassle. We're not making any money here. Rolly's is stuffing us down the tubes."

"I don't need you in the insurance business." He glared at her.

How could she expect him to be friendly? After

all, she had left him and moved in with Deb. She looked away, then asked about their younger daughter. "How's Marge?"

"Haven't you talked to her?"

"She won't talk to me."

"Chris will be home this weekend," he said, referring to their other daughter.

Amy's voice shook; she was perilously close to tears. "Chris talks to me when I call her. She's polite and distant."

John shrugged. "I'm sorry. I can't make them talk."

"I know. Can you stay until Leonard comes in?" The phone rang; she snatched up the receiver.

"I need a truck," said the voice. "I'm moving to Michigan."

"Where in Michigan?" She reached for the rate sheet.

"I hate men sometimes, Deb. I wish you'd come work for me. You'd be good with the people; I know you'd be good with the equipment." Amy warmed to the subject. "How about this summer when school lets out?" Deb taught social studies at one of the high schools.

"How would that look, Amy?" Deb appeared in the kitchen doorway, wiping her hands on a towel.

Amy propped her feet on a footstool while the rest of her sprawled on the sofa. "I'm so tired. I thought the winter would give me a rest and I'd be ready for spring," she complained.

"Well, it wasn't the easiest winter, honeybuns. Let's eat."

Amy groaned as she rose from the davenport. "I ache all over. Wet as it was, tractors and tillers and thatchers still went out. The lawn and garden craze is on. They'll all plant early and the stuff will freeze. Some guy insisted on renting a thatcher after I told him it was too wet to do what it should, and of course he didn't want to pay for it when he brought it back because it didn't do the job."

"I'm not sure I want that kind of summer," Deb remarked. "Did you have enough help?"

"John came in this morning. He's hardly been there since I moved out of the house. It was a good thing, too. I needed him. What do you say about helping this summer?"

"I'll think about it. Do you want a salad?"

Amy trailed Deb into the kitchen. "I'll make it. That's what I do best — food-wise, that is."

"You have your special talents."

Amy wrapped her arms around Deb and kissed her neck, then took Deb's earlobe between her teeth. "Do we have to eat? I want to fuck."

"Maybe later and don't use that word."

"It's so perfectly, wonderfully crude." She opened the refrigerator. In the freezer with the vodka was a plastic bag with rolled reefers. "I forgot we had these. Let's have one after dinner. Let our hair down. What do you say, babe?" She remembered how Deb had been turned on the last time she smoked dope, and she hoped there would be a repeat performance.

But Deb remained elusive sexually as she often

did. Amy fumed silently. If she said anything, Deb was likely to pack herself off to bed. It didn't seem fair. She herself was always willing and eager to please — why did she have to wait for Deb to make the move? Taking turns with the joint, they listened to music, then got into a hot tub.

"Why don't you want it?" Amy asked when she could stand it no longer. Deb glared. "Forget it," Amy said. "It doesn't matter. I don't want it either." And she realized that was the truth. What she wanted was Deb to want her. She was annoyed now, the evening ruined for her.

John tossed that night as if some part of him knew what his wife was doing. Yet he realized that his marriage to Amy had foundered on his lack of attention. Amy had warned him through the years not to neglect her, had begged for his presence, then announced her intention to leave after twenty-four years of marriage when she saw no change in sight unless she made it.

Shortly after one a.m. he switched on his bed light and picked up the latest Michael Crichton book. He turned the radio on to quiet jazz. At the knock on the door he looked up over his reading glasses, surprised to see Marge.

"Hi, Dad, saw your light."

"Well, how are you, kid?" She was lovely — tall, slender, honey-blonde hair, large gray eyes, freckles lightly sprinkled over her nose and cheeks, a sensual mouth, and straight white teeth. A taller version of Amy. He smiled. His own hair was light brown and his eyes were hazel. The girl looked like him, too. "It's late."

"I know. Matthew and I had a late dinner, then took in a show."

"Your mother asked about you today."

Marge looked at the wall above her father's head at the pictures there of herself and her sister, Chris, and her brother, David. She said nothing. She would not discuss her mother.

John worried about Marge; Amy worried about Marge; Marge's sister and brother worried about her. No one could draw her out; no one knew what she thought about Amy. She did talk to a therapist, but family members weren't privy to those conversations. " 'Night, Dad."

" 'Night, Margie." He returned to his book. If Amy were there, he would have to leave the room to read if she wanted to sleep. Being alone had its positive points. He sure could use a good lay, though. He wondered if he dared suggest it to Amy.

They should have waited until Friday night, Deb thought, as she turned south and Amy steered north the next morning. Her head felt stuffed with cotton. There were kids to deal with every day — talking, demanding attention, confessing problems, wants, needs, as if she had none of her own. She liked the kids; they liked her. That's why her room usually had two or three students in it, nearly always girls.

But the person who really needed her ear and support was Amy, and it annoyed her that she couldn't handle Amy's doubts and guilt, especially the way Amy's kids were ignoring their mother. She was part and parcel of it, but it hadn't been her idea to hurt Amy's family. She hadn't known Amy was married when she had met her. It didn't help that she now knew and liked John and Marge and Chris; and for that reason she didn't look forward to meeting David.

She knew Amy was angry about last night. A perversity she sometimes didn't understand caused her to reject Amy's sexual advances, and nothing Amy said or did could break down her resistance. Maybe she felt that gave her some control. All she knew was that she wouldn't analyze it — and she wouldn't dismiss it.

The rental store would be a madhouse. Cars were parked along the roadside waiting for the gates to open. Good, Amy thought, the busier she was today the better. She didn't want to think about Deb or Marge or John or Chris or Larry or whether she had made the mistake of her lifetime. It seemed like she couldn't please anyone, least of all herself. Today she'd make a superhuman effort to please the customers.

Seven-thirty, and no sign of Ted. Almost afraid to open the gates and let in all those people, she knew there was no way she could handle that kind of traffic. Still, she didn't have a choice. She slipped the Grand Am into the rear parking lot and closed the gate behind her, then walked around to the front and let the cars in. As she opened the doors to the building, Ted roared into the back lot in his Ford pickup. She sighed in relief.

Besieged with customers, Amy noticed a fifteen foot Ryder drive in and block the entrance.

"Maybe no one else will be able to get in," Ted said out of the corner of his mouth.

"No one can get out either," she pointed out.

As welcome as a knight in shining armor, Leonard stuck his head in the door and waved, then drove the Ryder to the fuel tanks. Amy silently blessed him for coming in without being asked. She checked in equipment, while Ted signed it out. Leonard could fill tanks, load and unload stuff, instruct renters in operating machinery, look over what was returned. The three of them could handle things if there were no deliveries.

"How'd you get along?" she asked a man who was returning an electric breaker hammer.

"Beat the hell out of me," he said.

Something about the tone of his voice caused her to study him. "Plug it in, will you?"

"Why? I don't need no more vibrating."

Walking around the counter, she took the hammer and plugged it in an outlet. There was a whirring sound when she pushed the switch. The ten gauge, fifty foot cord was still attached. "What happened?"

"Nothing." The man shrugged.

"Sounds like the motor's burned up. Did you use more cord than the fifty feet?" Distinctly she recalled telling him not to use more than the fifty foot cord.

"Had to."

"It's going to cost you."

"I had the damage waiver."

"I told you not to use more cord or higher gauge."

"The damage waiver should cover it."

Damn, she thought, why didn't people like him go to Rolly's. She ran a hand over her face to wipe away the anger. "The damage waiver doesn't cover negligence." The customers in line stopped shuffling and talking and gave her their unwanted attention. "I'll send you a bill for repairs."

"I won't pay it."

Laying the hammer on its side, she turned her attention to the next customer. The woman handed her a Ryder contract.

"You brought that fifteen-footer in?"

"Yeah." The woman grinned at her.

Sometimes you like people instantly, Amy thought, smiling back into friendly blue eyes. She guessed the woman, Jane Benchley according to the contract, to be between Deb and herself in age. She was slender and tall with curly brown hair, and Amy was fairly certain the woman was gay, although she couldn't have said why. "Welcome to the north side of Indianapolis." She filled in the blanks of the contract and refunded the difference between the gas used and the deposit.

"Now if I can just find Ridge Road again," the woman said, "I'll be in good shape."

"I live on Ridge Road," Amy responded.

"Then maybe I'll see you again."

"Hope so and thank you." Amy watched Jane Benchley climb into the passenger side of a waiting Camaro. She strained but failed to see the driver.

Her attention fell on the next customer and she forgot Jane as, with falling heart, she checked in a broken rototiller. "What on earth did you hit?"

"Didn't hit nothing. It just fell apart."

Amy stared at the tiller and then the man. She sighed. It was possible. Rototillers took a terrible beating.

Parking in back, John stepped out of the Bronco and released Grit. Tongue lolling and tail wagging, the dog bounded off in search of Amy. John paused to help Leonard, who was swamped with returned and outgoing equipment.

John liked to work outside when he could. That was why he had helped Amy start the rental business — that, and his enduring interest in machinery. But it was the insurance business that paid the majority of the bills, so he spent most of his time there.

They worked in harmony until afternoon, when business slackened and Ted left for lunch. John went out to bring back McDonald's hamburgers and fries. He and Leonard and Amy snatched bites between customers. Amy wired a trailer with a Pepsi balanced on the tongue of the trailer. The renter was so impressed with her ability to attach the right wires together that she was insulted. He would think nothing of it if she were a man. She glanced at John, who had coveralls over his good clothes and was greasing a loader tractor. Leonard was in the workshop fixing the broken rototiller. She thought of old times when she and Leonard and John had worked together sometimes late into the night. Then she and John had something in common — work.

"You're something else, lady," the renter commented as he climbed into his car after checking out the lights on the trailer.

"Thanks," Amy said, snatching her Pepsi off the tongue. "Hope the trailer works out for you."

"I want to sell," she said as she passed John on her way inside.

"Then sell," he said. "I don't give a fuck."

"How do I go about it?"

"Advertise. How the hell do I know?"

She would. She'd advertise in the rental magazines. But what to ask?

John methodically greased the loader, then the tractor. He wouldn't help sell the place. He'd given her a business; how many men did that for their wives? She worked her ass off; he knew that, but he helped when he could. Everything she wanted she got, and she was never satisfied. He couldn't be with her all the time; he didn't ask her to go everywhere with him. Was she really sleeping with Deb? No, he said to himself. He couldn't believe that. He didn't want to believe it.

"Tell Chris to come in Saturday. She can work if she wants," Amy said before John left.

"I'll help," John said, removing the coveralls.

"Can you come in, Leonard? You were a godsend today. Did I thank you for showing up?"

Leonard nodded. "I'll work. What about you, hotshot?" he asked Ted.

"Have I got a choice?" Ted asked, spitting into his miniature spittoon.

"No choice," Amy said, caressing Grit's sleek head.

After the front door was locked, Amy gathered

the day's receipts to put them in the office safe. John followed her into the room.

"I wondered if maybe you might want to . . ."

Amy fiddled with the safe's lock. "Can you open this, John?"

Bending over the safe, he opened it easily.

"Thanks." Don't ask, she pleaded silently; don't make me say no.

He didn't but, as he left, he wondered if it would really be so difficult to do what they'd done so well for twenty-four years. He slammed the Bronco into gear and listened to Grit's toenails scrabble on the floor for grip. Damn her, he thought, maybe he wouldn't help Saturday.

The Subaru hummed toward home the long way, its sunroof open, the radio cranked up. Deb leaned back against the seat, tapping out the beat on the steering wheel. Late afternoon sunshine warmed her. She could smell spring, the earth drying out. Forsythia outlined lawns and driveways with its yellow blooms, magnolia trees sported pink flowers, crabapple trees budded in yards, tulips and daffodils littered the landscape with bright colors.

Driving home gave her time to unwind. Tomorrow was Saturday. It couldn't arrive too soon. If teachers were forced to teach longer than nine months, she would have to find another occupation. Come April she was always threatened with burnout, and this year she had promised to help with track. But it worked well time-wise because Amy was seldom home before six-thirty.

A red Camaro turned onto Ridge Road in front of her and parked in the driveway across the street. Sports cars were Deb's passion. One of her goals was to someday own a Porsche 911 or a Mercedes coupe. She slowed to see who got out of the Camaro. The women emerged, unlocked the trunk and removed suitcases which they carried into an apartment.

A honk from a passing car made her jump. She shook her fist at Amy, who grinned and waved. Hearts really do leap and jump and drop, Deb thought, just like in books. Hers soared a little as she followed Amy's Grand Am into the parking lot.

"How are you, lady? What were you looking at?" Amy stood and stretched, talking over her car roof at Deb who parked next to her.

"We've got new neighbors." Deb got out of her car.

"You're so damn nosy. Were they driving a red Camaro? I was so busy looking at you I didn't notice."

"Yes. Do you know them?"

"This really nice, really cute lady brought a Ryder in today. Said she lives on Ridge Road and then she drove off in a red Camaro."

"Hmmm. Is she or isn't she?"

"My guess is yes she is."

"Too bad we don't have a nice casserole to take over."

"I'm not going to whip one up tonight. Look at me. I'm a mess." Amy walked around her car to help Deb carry in the inevitable papers she brought home and the clothes she changed out of for track.

"How did you get into such a state?"

"Follow me around some day and you'll find out. It's that kind of business. I told John I wanted to sell."

"I'll fix drinks if you want one." Deb strode into the kitchen. "I thought maybe I could work with you Saturday."

The possibility of Chris and John showing up at the business and finding Deb there flashed like a moving picture through Amy's mind.

"But I can't. There's a track meet tomorrow. I hoped you could come."

"I'm sorry, Deb. I'd love to, I really would, but I have to work. It will be the busiest day of the week. How was your day?"

"Good. I already know yours was busy. Want to tell me about it?" She turned toward Amy, pushed her against the counter, and ran her hands under Amy's pullover shirt. Leaning forward she kissed her, pulling softly on her lips with her own. They could get lost in kissing — watching each other's mouths with crossed eyes, breath quickening.

Tonight Amy took a couple steps sideways, slipping out from Deb's arms. "I need a shower."

"I don't mind." Deb reached for Amy again.

"I've got to at least wash my hands."

"Hurry back." Deb turned to the drinks, feeling a little thwarted.

In the bathroom Amy studied her face in the mirror. Forty-five, she thought, and starting a new life. Crazy. She had washed her hands and face before leaving work. It was the need to escape Deb, the need to say no for once, not to turn into passionate mush in Deb's hands, that had sent her fleeing to the bathroom. Running from herself, she thought. Where the hell was her backbone? She made a face in the mirror, then noticed Deb behind her setting a drink on the counter, turning her around.

"What is it?" Deb asked.

"Nothing. I'm hungry, aren't you?"

"Okay, we'll eat first."

"Wouldn't you like to take a walk or something after dinner? It's such a nice night."

Deb emitted a throaty laugh. "Sure, I can wait."

Already her knees were weakening, along with her crumbling resolve to resist Deb. Sometime soon she had to get a handle on this relationship and some control over it. It wasn't fair that Deb always called the shots. A pearl of resentment formed in her core.

"What are you thinking?" Deb asked.

What Amy was thinking would start an argument or worse — Deb's silent anger treatment. Amy shook her head. "Nothing. What are you thinking?"

"You now what I'm thinking," Deb replied, putting her hands under Amy's shirt again.

Amy's skin tingled as it always did when she felt Deb's intimate touch, as if Deb gave off minute jolts of electricity through her fingertips. She tried to move away, but Deb's arms slid around her and held her. She turned her head so that Deb caught only the corner of her mouth in a soft, urgent kiss. Amy's pulse pounded along with the desire tugging in her groin. Still, she offered no help when Deb removed their clothes and lowered her to the bed. Deb's mouth brushing her neck and breasts, belly and thighs, sent involuntary shivers of pleasure through

Amy and galvanized her into action. She could no longer pretend indifference when she knew how wet she would be when Deb reached between her legs. Rolling toward Deb, she gave in to passion.

Light from the street cast shadows in the room. Hands behind her head, Amy lay motionless, unwilling to disturb Deb who lay face down on her pillow, one arm thrown heavily over Amy's ribs. Glancing at her lover, Amy smiled. She envied Deb's talent for sleep. When Deb's head hit the pillow, she could be gone within seconds while Amy lay awake and restless. Lifting Deb's arm and placing it next to her, Amy rolled onto her side.

There were so many uncertainties in her life — her kids, the business, John — any one of which could keep her awake nights. The rental insurance would come due in two weeks, the interest on the $85,000 note in three weeks, payroll every week, the monthly bills next week. The kids were furious with her for leaving their father, more furious because they suspected she was living in a lesbian relationship. How the hell was she supposed to sleep?

II

Amy's three kids were discussing her. Chris and David had arrived in time to go out to dinner with John and Marge. Now the girls sat cross-legged on one side of Marge's double bed while David sprawled on the other half.

David and Chris were twins adopted when they were infants. Chris — short and small and dark with large, brown, beautiful eyes — was soft spoken and delicate. She gave the impression of fragility but her core was steel. David was also slim and dark with the same eyes, except at five-feet-nine he stood six inches taller than Chris.

"I don't believe it," David said angrily. "Just because she's living with this woman doesn't mean they're queer."

"I don't want to discuss it," Marge said. "It's done. Why talk about it."

"Oh, Marge, you have to face certain things, you can't ignore everything you don't like," Chris said with exasperation. "Ignoring something doesn't make it go away."

"I'm going to leave if you talk about it any more." She jumped to her feet.

"All right," Chris said crossly. There was no one else with whom she felt she could talk about her mother. Of course it was easier to ignore it, which was what she did most of the time. But sometimes, especially late at night, she would suddenly go rigid and sweaty and hot at the thought of Amy and Deb, and then her heart pounded so madly it frightened her.

"I'm going to see her tomorrow. She doesn't know I'm here." David smiled faintly. He rose on an elbow. "She's still our mother, you know, no matter what." Whenever he saw Marge he envisioned Amy; they looked so much alike. Many adopted children wanted to know their real parents, but not him. Had he been granted a wish it would be that Amy and John were his natural parents.

Marge stated, "She's not my mother."

The anger in Marge's voice chilled Chris. This fury in Marge was akin to a volcano erupting periodically. "It's late. What do you say we hit the sack," she suggested.

David went to his old bedroom. Chris stayed with Marge. They had shared a room during their growing years. Chris had taken their twin beds when she moved into an apartment in Milwaukee, and Marge had inherited her parents' double bed when they bought a king size. The sight of John lying alone in that enormous bed caused Marge so much pain she seldom looked in on him at night. It made her want to kill her mother, to shake her, to slap some sense into her. How could she leave them? Tears slid silently down her face and she turned away from Chris, who stared at her sister with stricken eyes.

Marge slipped between the sheets and turned her back to Chris. Her body shook in spasms. Chris gathered Marge in her small arms, pulled her close, and buried her face in Marge's hair. A terrible sadness gripped her and tears wet her face and Marge's hair. They fell asleep lying so close they looked like one, tears drying on their faces, mouths open because they couldn't breathe through their noses.

Knowing his three children were in Marge's room, John had put his ear to the door before going to bed. He had heard some of their conversation, but not much because he hadn't listened long. He remembered Amy's passionate nature, how she had enjoyed making love, more than he had. His loss. But another woman? He doubted it.

Stretched out on the bed he recalled dinner with the three kids. They had laughed at each other until they choked. It was great to have them home. He and Amy had been so excited when they had adopted the twins twenty-two years ago, as thrilled with them as they were later with Marge. They felt the twins had made Marge possible.

Amy probably hadn't thought leaving would cause the kids to reject her, because he sure hadn't. Actually, the two girls were doing a bang-up job of ignoring their mother, but not David. John had sometimes been jealous of the closeness between David and Amy. Chris, though, cared for them equally, but she had been such an independent little bugger. John grinned to himself, thinking she still was.

Early, as the sun first poured light into the room, Marge rose and pulled on her exercise clothes. Chris stirred and awakened.

The two girls let themselves out into the cool April morning. Grit joined them on the lawn. While they stretched, he cavorted happily, throwing twigs in the air and attempting to catch them. Mist still covered the grass and dewy webs, connecting strands of grass and bushes, quivered delicately.

"Ready?" Chris asked after bending several times and touching fingers to feet and head to knees.

Marge nodded. The need to move possessed her; only then was she at peace. She pushed until the pain in her legs and lungs threatened to incapacitate her. The dream-like beauty of April met her eyes on every side as she and Chris loped along the streets on the far north side of Indianapolis. Pink petals blanketed the ground under magnolia trees. Flowering crabapple trees were a blur of hazy pink and white, redbuds an accent of color in just greening woods. Her own breathing and Chris's echoed in her ears; their feet made a soft thudding sound on the pavement. A chorus of bird songs greeted the new day. Chris struggled to keep up, and Marge slowed her pace. At five-feet-eight inches Marge had legs much longer than Chris's.

"I'm going to see Mom today. Want to come?" Chris's words came in labored spurts. "I think I'll help behind the counter. How about it, Marge?"

"Let it go, Chris. I don't want to see her, I don't want to talk about her. You and David go. I'll stick with Dad."

"Hey, that's not fair," Chris panted, feeling her heart beat in her chest, hearing it in her head. "No one asked you to make a choice."

"I made a choice," Marge said savagely.

"Okay, Marge, you're only hurting yourself."

"Then let me do it, okay? I don't tell you what to do."

Chris broke to a walk. "You go ahead. My legs are cramping."

"Sure you'll be all right?" Marge ran in place, surprised at how small Chris looked to her. It was difficult to think of Chris as small when she loomed so large in Marge's mind as the older sister with the iron will. Marge had spent her younger years tailing Chris and David.

Watching Marge sprint out of sight gave Chris a weird feeling, as if Marge were running out of their lives. Chris turned and walked toward home. Budding branches of apple trees tunnelled the narrow drive. Chris vowed she would either run or ride her bike now that spring was here. She hadn't known her body was so soft.

A note on the bathroom mirror when she went in to shower said that her brother and her dad had gone to the rental store; she should come when she was ready. Stripping off her sweaty clothes she turned on the shower and stepped under the spray.

Marge ran until her legs started to give out and her lungs burned. Then she collapsed under a sugar maple and leaned her head back against the rough bark of the trunk. A mockingbird sang madly on top of a light pole across the street, fluttering upward into the air every few minutes as if in pure joy. No song pouring out of his throat was the same but an imitation of all the bird songs he had heard. Sometime he must repeat himself, she thought, but she didn't hear any replays. How she longed to be filled with the joy of spring, of just being alive, as she had been last year. Last spring she had worked her free days in the rental store with her mother. After work, they had often biked together. Marge's breathing eased. She started toward home, loping nice and easy.

She slammed the front porch door behind her. Turning on the radio to a rock station, she pulled her clothes off on the way to the bathroom. Sunlight flowed into the rooms. Her greatest fear was losing this house where she had grown up, something she had never thought about until her mother had left, which had been when Marge realized there were no permanent relationships.

They had all known something was wrong when her mother had been gone so many evenings and weekends. One day last August Marge had asked her mother if she planned to leave them. She hadn't understood why Amy laughed hysterically and asked her why she thought that. It didn't matter; Amy had left, and Marge was unable to accept her mother moving in with Deb, with whom she had spent those evenings and weekends when she wasn't home. Her mother — fun, attractive, young in mind and heart — had chosen a woman over her family. At that point Marge said "No" out loud, rinsed the conditioner out of her hair, and slammed the shower doors open. "No," she said again and put her mother out of her mind.

Bedlam reigned at the rental store. A beautiful Saturday, which Amy would have loved to spend biking or walking, brought renters out like flies to a carcass. Leonard and John and David worked the floor and yard while she and Chris handled the counter and Ted delivered.

David had greeted her earlier as if nothing had happened, as if she had never left home. It warmed her heart like a friendly hand closing around it when he grinned and grabbed her, as he always did, enclosing her in his strong young arms. She sniffed into his chest and wiped her tears away on his shirt.

"It's so good to see you, David." Her arms tightened around him. "I didn't know you were coming home." She laughed and released him to search through her pockets for tissue.

"I wanted to surprise you."

"Well, you did. Got any news?"

"Not really. The job's okay. Thought I'd help today. Mom, can we all go out to eat tonight?"

Amy glanced at John, who stood nearby watching them. He shrugged and raised his eyebrows.

"Sure," she said. "Marge too?"

David looked at his feet and performed a little shuffle. "No, probably not Marge."

"Oh, well the four of us then if Chris will go," she said in a small voice.

But not Deb, she knew, and wondered how Deb would react to being shut out. It would be a worry if Deb took offense. No matter how Amy turned someone was angered.

Chris had given her mother a quick squeeze from behind, an obligatory kiss on the cheek, and started to work the counter with Amy. Amy glanced at her daughter and noticed the same reserve in her eyes that she had felt in the embrace. Always tuned into her kids, Amy was even more so now that she expected their disapproval.

Deep within, Amy believed her kids would never completely forgive her for what she had done and was doing. There would always be an element of distrust in their feelings toward her. She had spent their growing years instilling values in them, values they must think she herself was disregarding.

A rap on the counter brought Amy's attention to the man standing before her with a cigarette hanging from his thin lips. Alan Young. She was displeased to see him; she didn't trust him. His shirt, unbuttoned and flung open, exposed to her and to Chris his puny pale chest and the tattoos emblazoned over each nipple — *sweet* over one, *sour* over the other. He was an evil-looking man with rotting teeth and greasy hair and one wandering eye, and Amy knew he would cheat her in the end. Already he was into the rental store for seven hundred plus dollars, and she had to hound him to get money out of him. "Hello, Alan, what can I do for you?"

"I need a crawler and backhoe." His gaze fastened on Chris. "Ain't seen you in a long time."

Amy fancied lust in his eyes and wanted to strangle him, as if just looking at Chris might rub dirt off on her. "When do you need the equipment?"

"My truck and trailer's outside there." Still staring at Chris, he pointed over his shoulder with his thumb. He slapped a wad of bills on the counter. "A couple days' rent there."

"Got anything to put on the bill?" Amy looked at the money with distaste.

"When I get done with this job, I'll have something. Ain't that enough now?"

Amy filled out the contract, counted the money — over six hundred dollars, nothing to sneeze at — and turned the contract around for Young to sign. "The men will help you load."

"Come work here more often, kiddo. You brighten up the place," he said to Chris before heading out the door.

Chris shuddered at his turned back.

The phone rang as Deb walked into the apartment. She picked up the receiver and set the bag of groceries on the counter.

"I've been calling all day." Amy sounded relieved.

"Why? You knew I had a track meet. Where are you?"

"At work. Deb, the kids are all home and want to go out to eat tonight."

"Oh, that's nice. I wish I'd known, though."

"I didn't know how to get hold of you."

Not keen on spending a Saturday evening alone, Deb felt a surge of anger and she tried to stifle it. "Don't you have to change?"

"I went home during the day and picked up some clothes. Look, I'm sorry, I really am, but I haven't seen Chris and David since Christmas and you know what Christmas was like."

Deb sighed. She did have Amy most of the time. It was hard knowing she was persona non grata with Amy's family, but it wasn't difficult to understand. "It's just that Jenny, one of the other coaches, invited me out to eat and I said no."

Amy pondered whether Deb would say no next time Jenny asked her to go out. Would Deb go out and leave her alone? "Oh, Deb, if I could just please everyone."

"Don't be melodramatic. No one expects you to please everyone," Deb snapped. "Go, have a good time. I think I'll meet the new neighbors."

Amy almost protested: *Without me?* But didn't. What right did she have? Instead she asked about the track meet.

A few minutes later, Deb strolled across the street and knocked on the door of the house of her two new neighbors. The Camaro sat in the driveway. One of the women threw the door open.

"I'm your neighbor across the street," Deb said,

smiling and pointing toward her apartment. "I believe you rented a Ryder and returned it to my roommate's business. My name's Deb Schmidt, and I wanted to ask you over for a drink, that is if you're not too busy." She took a deep breath.

"How nice, come on in." The woman swung the door open even wider. Deb slipped past her into the front room which was, not surprisingly, in disarray. "My name's Jane Benchley. Let me get my roommate. Paula," she called.

A slender redhead appeared from the interior. "What? Oh, I didn't know anyone was here."

Jane introduced Paula Tishner to Deb, who shook her hand. "Deb asked us over for a drink."

Back in her apartment, Deb removed three Lite beers from the refrigerator. "That Camaro's a nice car," she commented. "I love sports cars."

"Thanks," Jane said. "I love it too. It's not much good when it snows, though."

"Then we fall back on my Escort," Paula remarked.

Deb smiled. "I know what you mean. My roommate, Amy, drives a Grand Am. We have to have one practical car."

They talked about livelihoods next. Paula worked as a loan officer at a branch bank, and Jane was a physical education teacher.

They made an evening of it, returning to Deb's apartment after dinner. Deb was in the bathroom getting ready for bed when Amy walked quietly down the hall.

"I had a really nice evening," Deb said.

"Did you go out with the Camaro couple?"

"Uh huh. They're lots of fun. Did you have a

good time?" Deb leaned against the doorway, dressed only in an undershirt and panties.

"Yes, it's not quite like it used to be, though. Things are a little tense. Marge wasn't there, just John and Chris and David." She removed her dress slacks, then began unbuttoning the blouse.

Deb stepped forward and unbuttoned the shirt for Amy, whose eyes lit up with longing. Deb laughed.

"Why are you laughing?" Amy asked.

"You're always so eager."

Amy swallowed the quick retort. Two nights in a row of lovemaking were too rare to ruin with words. Her hands moved up Deb's arms and traced her collarbone. Leaning forward she kissed Deb's cheek, her neck, her lips, the hollow between neck and collarbone.

Deb yawned. "Let's go to bed, honeybuns."

The pearl formed another layer of hardness inside Amy. She dropped her hands to her sides.

As she did every morning, Amy awakened at six. Curled in a ball next to her, Deb slept on. A chirping sparrow sang monotonously in a bush outside the window. Amy rolled out of bed and onto her feet in one motion. She loved Sundays, the only day of the week she didn't have to work. It would be a crime to spend the day in bed.

Padding out to the kitchen she made coffee and went to the bathroom while the water dripped through the grounds. Then she retrieved the newspaper and took it and her coffee outside to the patio. Spring made enduring the cold sodden winters worthwhile, she decided as she turned her face to the sun while a soft breeze washed over her.

She dressed and took her bike down the road. She rode for exercise, eating up the miles with head tucked and legs pumping. She found herself in familiar territory near the home she had lived in with John and the kids. Braking in front of the brick house, she stood with one foot in the street and one on the curb. Not even Grit was in sight. But the house, a good four hundred feet off the road, was well hidden by trees and bushes. Why the hell was she here? This wasn't home anymore, even though her kids were in the house and so was John. She had alienated herself. If she wanted, she could go back and resume her old life; John was waiting for her to return.

Amy hungrily watched Marge carefully shut the door behind herself and Grit. She hadn't seen her younger daughter in weeks. Conscious of her status as intruder, she didn't stay long enough for Marge or the dog to spy her.

On her way back to the apartment she swung by the rental. With the front gate closed and locked, the building and yard appeared empty. As she pedaled past, she saw the rear gate ajar. Riding through the open gate, she noticed the side door also open. Shit, she thought. Her eyes took in the yard before she parked the bike. What had been there when she left last night?

There were gaps in the rows of small equipment inside the building, but the stuff could have been rented out. She thumbed through the contracts in the out-box while mentally recalling the inventory. It had grown beyond her immediate recall. She called John and asked him to drive over.

"What the hell are you doing there?" He sounded sleepy and annoyed.

"I was riding my bike; I rode past. We've been robbed, John."

"It happens."

"Well, shit, what kind of attitude is that?"

"You wanted to sell."

"I want to have something to sell," she snapped. Did he have to be so calm? She looked out the front windows at the blue sky. This wasn't how she had planned to spend her Sunday.

"Call the police."

She did so, and called Deb as well. Soon two squad cars drove in with John and Grit behind them in the Bronco.

"You carry the insurance?" one of the cops asked John.

"No, Harry, it's rental insurance; I don't carry it."

He and Amy had just completed a quick inventory. Missing were two new generators, a Ditch Witch trencher also new, a recently purchased Case loader tractor with trailer, a portable Miller welder, a 580D Case backhoe loader, and a brand new fold-down Starcraft camper.

"Some of the neighbors had to notice what was going on," Amy said. Thoroughly crabby, she was ready to snap at everyone. She wasn't sure how many tools were gone yet.

"Not necessarily, ma'am, but we'll check soon."

"Call the insurance company tomorrow, Amy," John advised her.

"Thanks, John I never would have thought to do that," she snarled. Her Sunday lay in ruins; Monday would be a mess; it always was and now she had to take care of this.

Two more cars drove onto the lot and David and Chris got out. "Good God, looks like a robbery," Chris commented, entering the building.

"Very astute," Amy remarked, wanting to bite her tongue off as soon as the words were out.

A new car drove through the open gate, another one close behind. "Saw the gate open. I thought you were closed Sundays."

"We are closed Sundays," Amy said, thinking this was turning into a parade. "Come back tomorrow," she said, close to the end of her patience.

"As long as you're here, would you rent me a tiller?"

Amy shook her head before he finished the sentence. "Sorry, come back Monday."

"What's the difference?" the man persisted. "You're here. Why not make a buck?"

"Yeah," the man in the other car said, "that's what I want too — a tiller."

"No, not today. Please leave," Amy said.

John looked at her, and she knew he was about to ask why not. She shook her head in warning; she would rent nothing today. If she rented to one, she'd have to rent to others.

"You heard the lady," one of the policemen said.

The two men left, promising to go to Rolly's from

then on, and David walked outside and shut the gate.

The police drove off; the kids left; John replaced the door lock and chained the gate. Amy headed home. It was two o'clock in the afternoon. She found Deb grilling chicken on the patio with Jane and Paula, who were sprawled nearby in lawn chairs.

"Thought you might be hungry. I told Jane and Paula about the rental being broken into. Is much missing?"

"Well, let's see," Amy said dejectedly, "about sixty-five thousand dollars worth of stuff is all."

"Holy balls," Deb exclaimed. "But it's all insured, isn't it?"

"It's sort of like having someone run into your car and you being inconvenienced because now you don't have car. Only it's worse because that equipment made money for you and now it can't until it's replaced."

Jane and Paula murmured their concern. "We've got a lot to do," Paula said.

"No, please don't go," Amy said quickly. "Company will be good for me. I need to get my mind off this. There's nothing more I can do until tomorrow, and I didn't get a chance to meet you yesterday. Of course, I met Jane on Friday." Amy told herself to shut up, to stop babbling.

"You were having a hard time Friday too," Jane remarked.

"Oh yes, that guy who burned up the breaker hammer. I forgot. One day runs into another. Can I get anyone anything to drink?"

She went to the kitchen, started to fix herself a gimlet, then changed it to just tonic. The phone rang.

"Hello, Amy speaking." She had nearly said Netzger Rentals.

"I'm going to keep the hoe and crawler a week." It was Alan Young.

He couldn't wait until tomorrow to call? And come to think of it how did he get the number? She asked him.

"I called your house, someone gave me this number. Don't you live there no more?"

She didn't answer the question. After all, it was none of his business. "Will you bring in some money tomorrow?"

"I told you I'd pay when I'm done with the job."

"Not good enough, Alan; I can't let you get further behind. Where are you working?"

"I'll call in a couple days." The phone went dead.

She stared at the receiver, a slow rage coursing through her. He'd done this before, disappeared with equipment, but he'd always paid in the end. The thing was she had known then where he was living; she didn't now. She hung up and took her drink to the patio.

The talk was idle chatter about cars, bikes, sailing. Jane and Paula owned a Zuma and offered to take Amy and Deb out on Eagle Creek Reservoir.

"I love to sail," Deb said. "Anytime, I'd really like to go."

Amy, unable to forget the stolen equipment or Alan Young keeping the hoe and crawler another week without paying, couldn't keep track of the conversation. The sun felt good, though, and it was pleasant just to relax and listen to the others having a good time.

"Next Saturday, how about then?" Jane suggested.

"I can go. Can you take the day off, Amy?"

"I doubt it. I'll try but this is the busiest time of year."

"Sunday we have to visit Jane's folks before they disown her," Paula put in. Her red hair shone like copper in the sun.

"I'll fix lunch to take along," Deb volunteered.

Fuming a little, because Deb was going to spend Saturday on the water with these other women, Amy struggled to conquer what she knew was an unjustified anger. Who wouldn't rather spend the day sailing than working?

"We'll bring the liquid refreshments," Paula said.

It was always annoying to be left out, Amy thought, and there was all this other stuff going on that she had to deal with. Don't blame Deb, she told herself. But how could she act as if nothing had happened, as if she'd forgotten the robbery, as if Amy weren't even there?

Perhaps sensing the undercurrent of anger in Amy toward Deb, Paula and Jane left before the last light of day vanished. Faint purple bruised the sky in the west, pale pink puffy clouds floated in the east, and a sliver of moon hung low, ready to set.

III

With Paula and Jane gone, Amy said, "Well, I'm off to bed."

"Already?" Deb asked with surprise. "Sit with me awhile. You haven't really told me what happened at the rental."

"You haven't really asked."

"You're angry, aren't you? You're mad because I'm going sailing next weekend."

Just like Deb to pin her to the wall, Amy thought. She wiggled a little. "I'm upset. It's not every day I lose over sixty thousand dollars worth of equipment."

Deb reached out and placed a hand on Amy's knee. "I'm sorry Amy, I really am. And if you want me to work Saturday instead of sailing, I will."

Amy laughed softly. "Sometimes I think you look inside my head. No, you go sailing. I just wish I could go too."

"Tell me about this morning, about what happened at the rental."

After filling Deb in on the details, Amy told her about Alan Young's call.

"He's done this before, disappeared with equipment, but he's always paid in the end and returned the stuff."

"Then the most obvious question is why did you rent to him?"

"Good question. Greed, I guess. I need the money." She needed all the money she could lay her hands on. "Now I'm short equipment with the busiest season of the year coming on." The seed was sown, though, and Amy wondered if Young was indeed responsible for the missing equipment.

The light slowly disappeared from the sky, the color with it, and stars stood bright in the velvety black. "Let's hit the sheets," Deb suggested. "Come on."

In bed, offering comfort, she held Amy close, her hands wandering absently over her body. "You feel good, Amy — so soft, so smooth."

Amy smiled in the dark and responded half-heartedly by running her fingers through Deb's dark curly hair.

Deb grasped the elastic of Amy's panties and tugged gently. "Take these off."

"Not tonight."

"Tonight, now," Deb insisted. "It'll take your mind off things, give you something else to think about." She slid a hand inside the bikinis and worked them off.

"You don't take no for an answer, do you?" Amy asked with interest, noting how different it was when Deb refused her.

"Did you mean it?" Deb's hand moved over Amy's breasts and ended up between her legs, fingers slipping gently over the silky warm wetness. "You don't feel as if you meant it."

Amy didn't answer. Instead she removed Deb's undershirt and panties. She sighed when she felt the smooth soft length of Deb's body against her own. It was true that she forgot everything but the act itself when they made love.

In Matthew's bed Marge rose to meet him. The day Amy had moved in with Deb, Marge had capitulated to Matthew's insistent sexual overtures, but unlike Amy she had trouble concentrating on lovemaking. It had been more fun when all she and Matthew did was tease each other; then sometimes she had come. She'd go home tonight and give herself an orgasm.

Matthew wanted her to move in with him. She had refused to leave her father and home, in her mind protecting them both with her presence. Besides, she valued her independence. She had lived with another boyfriend the summer following her sophomore year of college and had been badly burned. She wouldn't do it again unless she was crazy about the guy, and she wasn't in love with Matthew. He was fun, someone who could distract her.

"Did you come?"

"What?" She wished he wouldn't always ask her that because she rarely did.

"You didn't, did you?"

Actually, she hadn't realized it was over until he had asked her the question. "It was nice," she sidestepped the question. "But unfortunately I have to go home and study. Finals are coming up. God, I'll be glad when it's all over."

"Graduation in less than a month."

"And no job yet."

"You'll get a job. Good looking girl like you." He propped himself up on an elbow. His penis drooped to one side.

Marge glanced at it, noticed the wetness, and crinkled her nose. His last remark annoyed her. He should know better than to make chauvinist comments to her. "Looks shouldn't make a difference."

"They help, though."

She pulled on underpants and slacks, then put on her bra and shirt. The thought that Matthew was a mistake popped anew in her mind. He was too proud of himself.

"Got to go," she said, bending over the bed for a kiss.

He dragged her down next to him and squeezed her.

"Let me go, Matthew. My clothes will be wrinkled." She pulled away.

He walked her to the door of his apartment. "Wish you'd take a shower with me."

"Maybe next time. See you tomorrow." She wished she had taken a shower too. In lieu of one she had stuffed tissue in her panties to absorb the wetness. That was the bad part of sex, she reflected, the smell and wetness afterward.

When Marge walked in the back door, John was watching television, taking up the length of davenport.

"Hi, Dad. What's on?"

"Some miniseries. It's not bad. Listen kiddo, what do you want to do for graduation?" Sometime someone had to broach the subject. Was Amy to be included in the festivities?

"I'll think about it." She didn't want Amy there, but ignoring her mother was difficult. "First I have to pass finals."

She escaped to her room, a haven when she was in distress. She turned on National Public Radio but it reminded her of her mother, so she changed the station to rock, got her books out and settled on the double bed, pillows propped around her.

"Take your laps," Deb hollered to the girls on the track team. Thinking she could use some exercise herself, she fell in a few meters behind the pack of running girls. Her body responded favorably to the easy pace she set; it felt good. "If I can keep up with you, you're going too slow. Pick it up," she shouted.

The girls turned and grinned at her. "We didn't know you could run, Ms. Schmidt," one of them said. "We just thought you blew the whistle."

"Just for that add ten more laps," she called with an answering grin.

It was a gorgeous day, pleasantly warm and sunny. As she rounded the end of the track, she looked off to the right and stopped dead. Marge stood on the sidewalk staring at her. Marge's face, especially the gray eyes, reminded her of a storm cloud. Did the girl want to talk or was she just watching Deb? Struck cold by the possibilities, Deb automatically stretched out a hand, and Marge turned to leave. "Wait," she called.

Marge looked back over her shoulder as she sprinted off. She hadn't been seeking out Deb; she had been running past and seen the woman on the track.

Before the separation Marge had liked Deb. It was easy to like Deb, because Deb liked people and she especially liked Marge. Although Marge knew Amy was responsible for her own actions, still, Marge felt betrayed by Deb. Seeing her had almost precipitated an encounter, and Marge could not imagine such a meeting. What would she say? "Leave my mother alone?" That would be too stupid. No one had forced Amy to do anything.

Her gaze fixed on Marge's disappearing back, Deb felt for the first time the pain she and Amy had inflicted on Amy's family. The girl's distress was so evident on her face. This must be what Amy dealt with whenever she thought of her kids and John. John wasn't blameless, although he certainly had been more than decent about the separation, but the kids were victims. It didn't matter that they were supposedly grown up. Their parents were still the center of their lives, a couple of anchors. Deb didn't want to come to terms with the results of her actions. It was easier to ignore how their love, hers and Amy's, affected others. Anyway she couldn't give Amy up.

The pack of girls had rounded the track and were nearly on her, forcing her to put Marge out of mind. "Move it," she yelled, as they passed her and she fell in behind them again. Running could be good therapy, she thought, and wondered if that was why Marge ran.

Monday was always a busy day for Amy. The Monday report had to be completed and sent to Ryder, Saturday's equipment checked in, pick-ups and deliveries made: contractors were big Monday renters. And, of course, she had to deal with the insurance agency about the stolen equipment, and they weren't thrilled about what she had to tell them. She stressed the need to replace the missing machinery as soon as possible. One of their agents would come out to discuss details with her on Tuesday. It was a frustrating day, more so because Alan Young kept cropping up in her mind. He did not call during the day or bring in any money.

"I'll be glad to see today end," she said to Ted late in the afternoon.

"I wonder who did it," Ted mused. "It had to take a lot of time to load all that stuff. Somebody must have seen it."

"My thoughts exactly. The equipment will probably be found too late to do us any good."

Fifteen more minutes and they could lock the gate. A couple with two small children in tow walked through the front door. She and Ted eyed them.

"Ten to one they want a camper, and I can't stay tonight," he said.

Ted locked the gate while Amy demonstrated how to set up and crank down the camper. Then she took care of the paperwork before wiring the Starcraft to the couple's car. It was just her luck the car was foreign, she thought wryly. Foreign cars required an adaptor into which she had to connect turn signal wires and brake light wires, so they came out as one wire for each side to match the trailer wiring. As she worked, the two kids climbed from one machine to another, shrieking and shouting. She didn't leave the grounds until seven.

"Where have you been?" Deb asked when Amy let herself into the apartment.

Amy told her. "One of these days I'll get sued because some kid got hurt." She plunked down on the sofa. "I'm starved, woman."

"I'll fix something to eat. Want a drink first?"

"I'd kill for a drink." Amy followed Deb into the kitchen, put her arms around her and kissed her on the cheek, then buried her face in Deb's neck. "And how was your day?" Her voice was muffled.

"Busy. I saw Marge today."

Amy's head came up. "Where?"

"She ran past the track and stopped. Such anger, Amy, I've never seen such anger."

Leaning back against the counter, Amy sighed. "I know. I'm sorry, Deb."

"Why?" Deb asked, surprised.

"That you had to see it. Sometimes it doesn't seem fair for you to be involved."

"Why not? I am involved." But she didn't want to be. "It's tough enough on you. You shouldn't have to face it alone."

"You didn't know what it would be like, did you?"

"Did you?"

Amy nodded. "I think so."

"Are you sorry?"

"I'm sorry I hurt them. They didn't deserve it. I just couldn't help it." She shrugged, thinking how weak that sounded. It was difficult to shake the belief she had been wrong to pursue her happiness at the expense of others.

"A Catch-22."

"That's what it was."

"You know, Amy, if you ever want to go back, I won't stand in the way."

"Don't talk that way, Deb," Amy snapped. "I don't need to hear that. Besides you wanted me to leave."

"I want you to be happy." Deb handed a drink to Amy.

Amy stirred the liquid absently and then took a long drink. "You wanted to be happy too. Remember how unhappy you were when we were apart?"

"I didn't know until I saw Marge today what it must be like for them."

"Let's not talk about it right now. I'm going to take a shower." She carried her drink down the hall to the bathroom.

Water cascaded down on Amy, relaxing her tired muscles and nerves. Her life right now was hard but it was her own choosing. Making the choice had been the hardest of all, the most difficult decision of her life and one she had never before considered making. But she hadn't been able to live with the duplicity anymore, and, unable to give up Deb, she had chosen to leave John.

He was a mystery to her. She was grateful he hadn't attempted to keep her, but she didn't understand it. She would have raged had he left her, had she loved him.

Telling the kids had nearly undone her. Marge had reacted with tears and exercise, Chris with perplexed questions, David with confused silence. During Christmas, they had all made a determined effort to put a good face on the season. But when she had moved in with Deb, Marge had cut her mother out of her life — perhaps because she had asked Amy for the truth and Amy had denied her relationship with Deb, unable to admit it at the time. If one of her family asked her now, she would tell it like it was.

Stepping out of the tub she dried herself and dressed in sweats. She used the blow dryer on her hair before brushing it and examining it for gray strands. They were hard to discern among the dark blonde, but they were there.

Warmed up barbecued chicken and a tossed salad

were on the table when Amy joined Deb in the kitchen. "That really looks good. Of course, shoe leather would look tasty right now."

"Thanks for the compliment," Deb remarked dryly.

"What is so nice is someone making dinner for me."

"You know I like doing things for you."

"So do I, sweetie, for you." Amy turned on the public radio station. Strains of Rachmaninoff filled the room. "Isn't this pleasant?"

"Want some wine?"

"Unless you want to ride bikes after dinner."

"It's kind of late, isn't it?"

"I guess. I got plenty of exercise today anyway."

The phone rang. They looked at each other before Amy got up to answer it. Answering to Amy's family was awkward for Deb.

"I got a problem, Amy." It was Alan Young.

"What?" Her heart dropped like a stone. Then her adrenalin kicked in. If he damaged the equipment and didn't pay for it, she'd kill him. "Where are you working?"

He ignored the question. "I bled this hoe and it still don't start."

"I'd send Ted out to look at it if I knew where it was. Did you run it out of fuel?"

"Yeah, but I filled it and bled it."

"Just tell me where it is."

"I bled the fuel filter, the injectors, the injector pump."

"It's got two fuel filters," she said automatically and could have kicked herself for telling him. But she couldn't believe he didn't know that.

"That's it then."

"Where are you working, Alan? I'll send Ted out."

"I'll bring in some money soon." The phone went dead.

Furious, Amy slammed the receiver in the cradle.

Deb jumped. "Jesus, what now?"

"Alan Young. He ran the backhoe out of fuel and he didn't even know it has two fuel filters. That's hard to believe with all the machinery he's rented."

"Well, I didn't know it either," Deb admitted.

Amy looked at her roommate and laughed a little hysterically. "Want to take a drive after dinner? I want to see if I can find where he's working."

Although Amy drove around new subdivisions until they could no longer see in the growing dark, they found nothing. "Well, it was a nice night for a drive anyway."

Deb took Amy's hand. "We can look tomorrow night and every night until we find wherever he took the stuff."

"We could look for a month and not find him or it," Amy remarked. She squeezed Deb's hand. "Thanks for riding with me."

The week flew by. Friday night Amy, so crabby she could hardly stand herself, listened to Deb singing in the kitchen as she prepared lunch for the Saturday sail. She thought Deb could be a little more circumspect with her anticipation; she didn't have to be so obviously happy. Unable to concentrate on anything, Amy threw the paper on the floor, stomped out to the patio, and slammed the sliding screen door so hard it jumped off the track. "Goddamn it all to hell," she said, then struggled with the screen.

One disaster had followed another all week. The insurance agent told her that settlement might take several weeks, that there would be some depreciation. Leonard was in bed with the flu and John too busy to help, so she and Ted had been shorthanded the past five days. When Ted made deliveries, she was alone in the store and besieged by customers. A family acquaintance rented a tractor and plow and drove the tractor into a tree, smashing the front end so the radiator had to be replaced and the entire front end taken to a body shop. Miracle of miracles, the acquaintance wasn't injured, although at the time Amy wouldn't have cared, but he had taken the damage waiver and reasoned he shouldn't have to pay the two-hundred-fifty dollar deductible. The tractor would be down at least a week, when she most needed it. She still had no idea where Young was working and had heard no more from him.

Staring out at the night, fists clenched, she knew there was no way on earth she could get out of work tomorrow. Hearing Deb's cheerful voice even on the patio, Amy walked around the building to the garage. Pedaling furiously, she rode into the cool night.

Her bike had reflectors and a headlight operated by a tiny generator which ran off the moving tire. The narrow weak beam of light reflected off the blacktop a foot or so ahead of the bike. It was akin to riding into a black wall which passing cars briefly lifted. Amy knew the drivers would be almost on her before they spotted the bicycle. A barking dog suddenly appeared from a darkened yard. She swerved, nearly into a passing truck. Heart pounding, she turned sharply back toward the berm and almost fell. Putting both feet on the gravel by the side of the road, she felt her pelvic bone crunch against the crosspiece running from the seat support to the handlebars. She grunted and yelled at the dog, who vanished into the night. Then she rode painfully toward the apartment.

Watching her approach, Deb stood in the road under a street light. "What do you think you're doing?"

"What does it look like," Amy snapped, riding past and putting the bike in the garage.

"You could have been hit by a car," Deb said angrily.

"I nearly was." Her crotch still hurt. She headed for the bathroom and the pain relievers. "Damn dog nearly bit me too," she hollered.

"You don't have to yell." Deb appeared in the doorway. "Why didn't you tell me you were leaving?"

"You would have tried to stop me. Besides you were having such a good time in the kitchen I didn't want to spoil it."

"Back to square one, aren't we? My going sailing tomorrow."

"And my working tomorrow." In the mirror Amy's hair looked a little wild. She tried to run her fingers through the tangles. Her vision shifted to Deb's angry reflection. "I'm sorry, Deb. It was stupid. I'm just so tired of work," she said to the reflection. "This week was so bad, I just don't want to go in tomorrow."

"Don't then," Deb snapped.

"I have to. I don't know whether Leonard will be coming in or John. That leaves me and Ted. It'll be bedlam."

"I'll help. I'll call Jane and Paula and tell them," Deb said.

"No, Deb, don't do that. I'd have to train you. There won't be time for that tomorrow." Amy turned and leaned against the sink. "God, I hurt myself when that dog came after me and I nearly rode into that truck. I hit my crotch on the bar."

Smiling crookedly, Deb said, "Let me see."

Amy gave a short laugh. "You won't be able to see anything. I think I better go to bed. I have to get up early."

Saturday dazzled with warm sunlight. Deb rode with Paula and Jane in the Escort which pulled the sailboat. All the windows were rolled down. "What a day, huh?"

Brightly colored sails dotted the reservoir in spite of the early hour. Paula backed the trailer into the water. They removed the straps from the Zuma and released the crank; the boat slid into the lake. Wading in after it, Deb helped Jane ready the craft to sail. Jane raised the sail and the three of them climbed into the boat, Paula at the rudder, Jane holding the sheet. Deb sat near the mast.

When Deb felt the wind catch the sail, pick the boat up and speed it over the sun dappled water, she made a decision. She had to have a sailboat. Later, burning in the heat of the sun, she stretched across the front of the boat, feet hanging off one side, hands dangling in the water on the other. It slowed the craft but both Jane and Paula had also immersed hands or feet in the waves to cool themselves. They took in the length and width of the reservoir before the day was over, sailing back to pick up lunch just after noon.

Deb couldn't nail down exactly why sailing was so satisfying. She took both the rudder and sheet at different times during the day. Maybe it was mastering the wind; maybe it was the excitement when the Zuma heeled in a strong gust; perhaps it was just being on the water in the elements. But the day was too short for her.

Forgetting everything except the tasks at hand, Amy gave up any hope of escaping early. Around noon, she instructed a man on how to operate a tractor and mower and he in turn gave directions to his teenaged son. The man was standing next to the running board in front of a rear tire when the boy let the clutch out. There was nothing she could do but holler for the boy to step on the clutch and pray he didn't instead stomp on one of the brakes. She stood just behind the father as the slowly moving rear tire caught his clothes and walked him into the ground. She was forced to wait until he was down far enough, so she could reach over his fallen body to depress the clutch with one hand and knock the shift stick into neutral with the other. Eyes huge in his white face, the boy on the tractor said nothing.

Amy glanced down at the man under the large tire, pinned on his back with legs and arms and head sticking out and moving. What should she do? Should she get a jack and raise the tractor tire? But that would take time.

The man met her eyes. "Get this thing off me," he gasped.

"Off, get off," she said to the boy and climbed on the tractor, put it in gear and slowly backed it off the father, who struggled to his feet before she could turn off the engine. His shirt was in shreds. Jumping down from the seat, Amy couldn't quite believe what had just happened. "Let me take you to the hospital."

"I'll be fine; I will, really. Thanks for getting that off me." He attempted a smile which quivered on his face. His hands shook.

"I'm sorry, Dad. God, I'm sorry," the boy said, looking as if he needed a good cry.

Bent forward slightly, his father patted the teenager on the back. "It's okay, Jim. It was an accident. Just take me home. Okay?"

Jim burst into tears.

His smile more like a grimace, the man addressed Amy, "I'll be back." He pushed the boy toward the car.

She made another attempt. "Please, you must have broken ribs. Let me take you to the emergency room."

"I'll be fine." He waved her away.

Ted was in the shop working on a broken rototiller and thatcher, so Amy climbed back on the tractor and parked it out of the way. Then she told Ted.

"I miss all the exciting stuff," he complained. "Why didn't you call me?"

Perplexed, she asked, "Why the hell would you want to see that?"

Several cars followed each other into the parking area. Neither she nor Ted had eaten any lunch and it was twelve-thirty. Standing in the warmth of the sun, Amy mentally pulled herself together and hoped nothing else would tarnish the day.

Later in the afternoon the man whose son had run over him returned alone and, brushing aside her protests, took the tractor and mower. "You saved my life," he said when he returned the equipment around closing.

"I'm certainly glad you think that." Never again would she stand in front of a rear tractor tire, she thought, nor would she permit anyone else to stand in such a dangerous place.

Deb was still gone when she reached the apartment, so she cleaned up and drove to the launching ramp at the reservoir and watched the boats. Jane took her for a sail before they loaded the Zuma on the trailer, and Deb rode with her back to the apartment.

"All day I missed you — every time we got a good wind, every time I saw something I wanted to share with you. It was great fun but nothing's quite complete without you."

Amy smiled and squeezed Deb's hand. In the picture part of her brain she saw the man pinned under the tractor like a bug on a board. For some reason, she laughed.

"I'm going to buy a sailboat someday," Deb told her.

"That much fun, huh?"

IV

Letting himself into the empty rental yard, John locked the gate behind the Bronco and parked near the workshop. He had spent the afternoon at an insurance conference in downtown Indianapolis and felt cheated out of the day. The cool workshop was like coming home, he had spent so many hours there. Opening the overhead door, he let in Grit and the remainder of the day.

The tractor that had tangled with the tree was waiting for its front end to be replaced. A new radiator rested against a front tire. John picked up the radiator and began to mount it on the supports. He was most at peace with himself when working with his hands. The radiator bolted in place, he turned on the television resting on top of the shelves along the back wall.

He started on the small equipment needing repair. The light slowly darkened as he worked. The phone rang often, but he didn't answer it. When they had had an extension in the house, it sometimes rang intermittently all night. Someone would call at three in the morning wanting to rent a Ryder truck.

It was a lonely way to spend a Saturday evening but not unusual. He remembered Amy railing at him for returning to the workshop nights: "Life is meant to have some fun in it, some time together." And he would end up in the workshop anyway. It was his way to relax.

On the way home he stopped at the Legion, leaving the Bronco windows open for Grit.

"Hey John, come have a drink with us," Keith Moody called from one of the tables. Moody, John's friend for years, was separated from his wife, whom he had stepped out on as often as possible, gaining Amy's strong dislike.

Moody introduced the women at his table. "This here is Marilyn Holder and Jenny Quellhorst."

Moody bought a round of drinks. He put a possessive hand over Jenny's. "Let's dance. I like that song." He swung Jenny out on a tiny space that served as a dance floor.

John was left to entertain Marilyn.

It made him nervous, knowing this woman might think he was available. But wasn't he? He leaned his arms on the table and met the woman's eyes. She had very pretty eyes, he thought, dark blue surrounded by black lashes, and she had a wonderfully sensual mouth. He realized he was staring at her and dropped his gaze to his beer.

"Well, what do you do, Marilyn?" Raising his eyes to meet hers, it dawned on him she must be somewhere in her early thirties, possibly even twenties. Too young for him. The thought crossed his mind that Deb was only thirty-two, if he remembered correctly.

She grinned. "I work for an advertising firm, Gleason and Turner. I write copy. Some local TV, some radio, some newspaper." She shrugged. "What do you do?"

"I run an insurance agency, Netzger Agency, not far from here."

"You carry my car insurance. Maybe we can discuss rates."

He laughed aloud and the sound startled him. "Maybe we can discuss some of those ads on TV. Are the rates too high?"

"Probably not. I drive a new Celica GT and I got caught speeding twice last year."

"Your insurance would be a little high then."

"I'm not complaining, really." Her eyes lit up when she smiled and dimples made fetching creases around her mouth.

Had he been alone too long? he wondered. But she was attractive, even though she probably wouldn't consider him anything but an old man. But some women like older men, he thought. Her hair, reddish brown and wavy, hung to her shoulders. He wanted very much to touch it.

Keith and Jenny startled John when they rejoined them. "You two gettin' acquainted?" Moody asked with a grin and John was reminded of why Amy disliked the man.

"Maybe you'd like to give Marilyn a ride home?" Moody suggested to him.

"Well, I've got the Bronco and the dog's in it. He's probably in the front seat."

"I don't want to impose." Marilyn appeared uncomfortable.

"I'd like to take you home. I didn't think you'd want dog hair on your clothes." John looked at her clothes and noticed for the first time what a nice figure she had.

"I love dogs," Marilyn said.

Stepping out in the spring night with an attractive young woman was heady business, John realized. He opened the passenger door, and there was Grit sitting on the seat as if he were a person. "Move it, Grit. Get in the back." Grit leaned forward and licked Marilyn on the face.

Grabbing the dog's large head, she laughed. "What a nice dog, such a friendly greeting."

"Go on, back seat, Grit," John ordered but he laughed too, and the dog turned and squeezed between the two front seats to the open back.

On his way back home with Grit once again on the front seat, John sang tunelessly to the songs on the radio. "Nice lady, huh, Grit?" He knew where Marilyn lived, her phone number, that she'd like him to call.

Marge, curled up in a corner of the davenport, was watching a video tape. "Dad, where have you been? I was worried."

"That's a switch. I stopped at the Legion on the way home. Did you have a good evening?"

"It was okay but I get so pissed at men."

John raised his eyebrows in mock surprise. "You sound like your mother."

Marge snorted. "Matthew can be such a jerk. He loves to talk about himself but never listens when I talk."

"Well, he's not the only guy in town, and they're not all like that. You going to tell him to take a hike?" John stuck his head in the refrigerator in search of food.

"Not yet. Too many things are coming up when I need a date."

Slapping some peanut butter on a slice of bread, John walked into the living room. "We've got to clean this place up," he commented and bit into the sandwich.

"You never noticed it needed cleaning before."

"Just because I didn't say anything didn't mean I didn't notice. We can do it tomorrow."

Staring at her father in surprise, Marge asked suspiciously, "What's going on, Dad?"

"Nothing. It's just time to clean."

"Okay, okay," she said, running the tape back to where it had been when her father and Grit had come home. "It'll be nice to have help." She had cleaned alone after Amy had left.

"Are you going to be shitty all day?" Deb glared at Amy. "Because if you are, let's go back home. I could spend the day in bed."

Amy snorted. The windshield wipers softly thudded back and forth, brushing away sheets of rain. Gusts of wind periodically rocked the car. "Sleeping, no doubt."

Deb crossed her arms and stared out the side window, her face a cloud of anger. "Look, can we start over? As long as we're doing this, let's try to have some fun. The weather couldn't be worse. I can't even see the hills."

"I can't see the road," Amy said and laughed a little. It was preferable to crying which was what she wanted to do. Then the wipers went out of sync and started crossing each other. "Look, Deb."

The two women laughed at the sight until Amy couldn't drive anymore and pulled over to the side of the road.

Amy saw the pickup truck in the rear view mirror just before it hit them, which was probably when the driver saw their car and tried to swerve around the Grand Am. The impact pinned Deb to the seat, snapping her head back against the head rest. The driver's side of the car took the direct blow and Amy's seat came loose and skidded forward toward the steering column. She lost consciousness when she heard her arm snap against the wheel a split second before her head hit it. How the hell could she work at the rental with a broken arm was her last thought before her mind clouded over.

Deb struggled to free herself from her seat belt. Glass lay everywhere, the windows broken, but Deb only saw Amy's blood. Vomit rose in her throat, and she swallowed convulsively. Never would she fight with Amy again, if Amy would just be okay. "Amy," she called, knowing in the emptiness of her heart there'd be no response.

A man stuck his head in the broken driver's window, his face white except for a bruised lump growing on his forehead. "Jesus, what were you doing parked in the road?"

"Call an ambulance and get me out of here, will you?"

The man wrenched open the door and struggled with Deb's seat belt, finally releasing it. "I think you should sit still and wait for help."

She couldn't leave Amy's side anyway, Deb realized, now that it was physically possible to get out of the car. "Can't we move her seat back some? She looks crushed."

People gathered around the wrecked vehicle. They managed to open Amy's door and shove the seat back half a foot, and Amy moaned a little.

Disoriented, Amy thought she heard Deb's voice and she tried to respond. In fact, she thought she said something; she heard her voice in her head telling Deb not to worry. Where were they? Why were they out in the rain in this strange place? She felt hands on her, heard strange voices talking to her, reassuring her, but she wasn't worried; she knew she'd be all right.

At the hospital in the emergency room Deb was asked about Amy's family. "We need someone from the family to admit her since she's unconscious."

She and Amy were so close physically and mentally, yet Deb could not be legally responsible for Amy. She could never be considered next of kin. That would be John, as long as he and Amy remained married, and Amy's children if the marriage was dissolved.

They cleaned Deb up, probed for glass, took X-rays, said they wanted to admit her until morning for observation. She agreed in order to be near Amy, but Amy was put in intensive care.

John silently studied the tiny cuts crisscrossing his wife's face, the darkening bruise on the right cheekbone, the broken arm now encased in a white cast. Marge stuck her head in the room every five minutes. "Come on in," John said every time he saw her worried face. She only shook her head and continued pacing the hallway. Amy would be moved out of intensive care as soon as she regained consciousness. John knew her life was not in danger. The arm was broken and she apparently had suffered a concussion, but there were no internal injuries and the cuts were all superficial.

The anger Marge felt for her mother had dissolved in guilt during the drive to the hospital, as she watched the rain and prayed her mother wouldn't die. Now, reassured Amy would live, Marge felt battered by the emotions she had fended off with her shield of anger. She yearned to hold her mother, to be held by her. Somewhere in the hospital was Deb, Marge assumed, perhaps badly hurt. Would Amy return home if Deb died? But did Marge want her mother to come home on those terms? The anger stirred again.

Sitting with arms hanging between his legs, John waited for the first signs of consciousness. He knew Amy would ask about Deb, so he had inquired. He hadn't quite given up on Amy, thinking it possible she would want her old life back. Last night he had realized other women might be interested in her place in his life. The phone call had pushed everything out of his mind except Amy's welfare, but now that he knew she was going to recover he allowed his thoughts to wander.

"John," Amy said. Her voice sounded strange in her ears, like someone else's. Her head pounded as if a separate entity. She didn't raise it, didn't move it; it hurt too much. "What's going on?"

"You had an accident. Do you remember?" He took her hand; it was limp and cold.

"Where's Deb?" she asked, suddenly recalling Deb had been with her.

"She's all right but under observation. You were hurt more than she was."

"I want to see her." She didn't believe him. He could be lying to keep her quiet.

"She is all right. I asked. You'll have to believe me. She'll be in to see you tomorrow when they release her."

Keeping her eyes open was an effort. She closed them briefly, then opened them to see Marge at the door for her five-minute check. "Marge." She smiled a little. "Is that Marge, John?"

"Come in, Marge," John commanded.

Obeying, she took a few hesitant steps into the room as if she were walking into a pit of snakes and saw her mother extend her unbroken arm. "Hi, Mom," she said, swallowing tears.

"Hi, sweetie, nice of you to come." The arm fell back on the bed.

The throbbing in Amy's head affected her vision, causing Marge to blur, and again she closed her eyes. She didn't see Marge crying.

"It's the concussion," John explained to his daughter. "She'll be much better in a few days."

Down the hall Deb's mother sat at Deb's bedside. "I'll stay at the apartment with you for a few days once you're out of here," her mother offered.

"No, Mom, I don't want to interrupt your life." Too much togetherness might bring on a fatal quarrel. "I'll be fine. I'll be at the hospital anyway with Amy most of the time."

"How can you drive all this way every night? You can't do that?"

It would be difficult, Deb thought. "Maybe they'll transfer her to Indianapolis."

"Don't she have a family of her own?"

"She's separated from her husband."

"That's too bad. Didn't I meet him once? Don't he run an insurance agency? Such a nice man. You should get such a nice man."

"Yes, he's a nice man," Deb agreed tiredly, her head beginning to ache. "Do you mind if I sleep a little?"

"Go ahead. Don't mind me. I'll just sit here and read the paper."

Deb escaped into sleep. Her last waking thought was that tomorrow she could see Amy.

The following morning, pushing open the door to Amy's room, Deb smiled when her eyes met Amy's. "God, it's good to see you, even if you do look a fright."

"You look pretty frightful yourself," Amy replied. "I wouldn't believe John yesterday that you were all right. The doctor had to tell me."

"You're the one who was out of it. I never lost consciousness." Deb pulled a chair near the bed and before sitting bent down and kissed Amy, then took her hand.

"What a rude shock, huh? I saw the truck just before it hit us. Did you?"

"No, it was a complete surprise." The accident ran through Deb's mind, bringing back the fear and shock. "I was so afraid for you and we'd just fought. I promised myself I'd never argue with you again."

Amy smiled faintly. "I'm so glad to see you." She squeezed Deb's hand.

Deb, still off from school, took Amy home three days after the accident. Amy's first act at home, after collapsing in bed, was to call the rental.

Ted answered. "How are you?" he shouted jovially. "I got some good news, couldn't wait to tell you."

"What?" She closed her eyes to rid herself of double vision and to ease the throbbing behind her eyes.

"Alan returned the hoe and crawler Monday."

"No kidding. That is good news. Were they in good condition?"

"Well, they were filthy and he'd stuck a stick in the injector pump 'cause the bleeder plug was gone, but otherwise they're all right. And he brought in a thousand."

"That'll help. How are things going without me?"

"Leonard and I are holding the place down. John shows up for a few hours every day to remind us there's a boss. Marge came in yesterday."

Suddenly Amy was crying. "I'll call later," she said.

"Sure, you rest now."

"Why are you crying?" Deb asked, crawling into bed and taking Amy in her arms. "God, I wanted to do this in the hospital. It's terrible when we can't even hold each other."

"Did I tell you Marge was at the hospital Sunday? I talked to the other kids on the phone. Told them not to come home because of this. Marge went to the rental store yesterday, according to Ted." She snuggled closer to Deb.

"I told you she'd come around," Deb said, kissing Amy's face gently. "Am I hurting you?"

Amy sniffed and shook her head gingerly, which made it pound harder. "It feels good. Just being close, being able to touch without jumping every time someone comes into the room. It's great."

They fell asleep holding each other, Amy feeling that their love had been strengthened by the reminder of the tenuousness of life.

"Dad's dating someone, Mom," Chris informed her mother.

Lying on the davenport with David sitting at her feet and Chris across the room in a chair, Amy was pleased the twins cared enough to visit the apartment. Without being asked, Deb had absented herself from the premises.

Amy had been unable to attend Marge's graduation or even the dinner after the event. A confrontation had been avoided because Amy wasn't well enough to sit up for long periods of time, and the accident had taken place two weeks ago. Amy would have gone to the ceremony had she not had an excuse, but it had been easier on everyone this way.

"Is he really? That's good," Amy said.

"Come on, Mom, you don't really want him seeing another woman, do you?"

"He has a right to happiness too, Chris. How can I complain?"

"You can't but you could change it by going back home."

"I can't. I'm sorry."

David held his mother's feet, kneading them lightly as if he needed to touch her, as if it hadn't occurred to him she could die until the accident. "Do you see two of me, Mom?"

She smiled at her son. "Sometimes. It's better than seeing one."

He grinned. "Are you better, though?"

"I am. Tell me about your dad's girlfriend."

"I haven't met her," David said.

"Neither have I, but Marge filled me in," Chris said. "She's fourteen years younger than Dad, attractive, intelligent. She writes advertising copy."

"Does Marge like her?" Marge had briefly shown her love to her mother and then retreated.

"Marge likes her and resents her at the same time. This is all very difficult for Marge."

"I know, Chris." When one of her kids patronized her, she was sometimes amused, sometimes annoyed. "Tell me about graduation."

"Dad videotaped it for posterity." David retrieved the tape from his car.

The three of them watched it together, the kids and John the principal parties on the tape. "Who took it?" Amy asked.

"Matthew, Marge's boyfriend."

"What's he like?" Amy asked.

"He's a nice guy," David said.

"He's a hunk but a little in love with himself," Chris added.

After the twins had departed, Amy played the tape again. She needed to sort her feelings about her family. The physical and mental distance between them disturbed her. Viewing the tape focused her attention on that gap. Because she could see no solution, she counted on time to bring forgiveness or some sort of acceptance from her children.

"Did you know John has a girlfriend?" she asked Deb hours later. Poking a straightened coat hanger inside the cast, she moved it around. The itching was driving her mad.

"You're not going to have any skin left, buns. No, I'm not privy to that gossip. Does it bother you?" Deb slid the patio door open and stepped out into the May night.

"No. I suppose you and Jane will be spending a lot of time together this summer since you both have the summer off." Amy followed Deb into the warm, sticky blackness.

"Do I detect a little jealousy?"

"Only because I can't be with you."

Staring up at the sky, they stood on the cool concrete. A half moon floated among the stars and appeared to drift in and out of wispy clouds. They reached for each other's hands.

John spent the first night at Marilyn's apartment nearly three weeks after they had met. Both considered it a blinding success. Amy had taught him what she liked in bed and he had been sensitive enough to learn. And Marilyn became a grateful recipient of his attentions. Aware he had taken Amy for granted, John gave this second chance more time. He enjoyed running his hands over Marilyn's body; it was so firm yet soft and smooth, reminding him of a larger version of Amy, and at first he kept Amy in mind when he made love to Marilyn. The novelty of lovemaking had disappeared from his and Amy's relationship years ago, but it reappeared with Marilyn. John found Marilyn replacing Amy in his thoughts.

He introduced Marge to Marilyn when he brought Marilyn home to dinner. John had enlisted his daughter's unwilling assistance in preparing the food. Marilyn pitched in and helped Marge in the kitchen while John grilled. She didn't hover near John. Closer to Marge's age than John's, she had no trouble talking to Marge, and several times John found them laughing over something.

"She's a gorgeous girl, John," Marilyn said, when he took her home.

"She looks like her mother," he remarked without thinking.

"Then her mother must be gorgeous," Marilyn replied without blinking.

"We're still married, you know, Marilyn. This isn't exactly fair to you."

"I'm a big girl," she responded. "But I'm willing to listen whenever you want to talk."

He didn't want to spill his suspicions about Amy. "Amy wanted to separate." He glanced at Marilyn's blue eyes and shrugged.

"You didn't want to?" she asked.

"No, not then, maybe now."

"She didn't give you a reason?"

"She said she was tired of being alone and now that the kids were grown she didn't want to hurt anyone but she wanted to leave." But how could it make sense to anyone without bringing Deb into it?

"What did she mean she was tired of being alone?"

"Well, our interests were different. She said there was no one else. I'm not sure I believe her."

"Does she live alone?"

"No, she lives with another woman."

Marilyn turned toward him, her eyes questioning, but she didn't speak and he didn't volunteer more information.

He started thinking divorce. But it was easier to think divorce than initiate proceedings. Financially he and Amy were cemented together. Together they owned both businesses, the house and furnishings, two vehicles. To settle with her he would have to come up with a fair amount of cash, which would mean selling some of the assets. And for what reason? He had no plans to marry Marilyn. Did he?

V

The third week after the accident, Amy knew she had to at least catch up on paperwork at the rental store. Only absolutely necessary bills had been paid, the Monday reports sent to Ryder, deposits made every few days to the rental account. Contracts had to be entered in the monthly ledger so that sales tax could be figured and a running account of income recorded for the accountant. The remainder of the outstanding bills needed to be paid and expenses entered. Inventory also had to be reordered. The paperwork gave her a nearly unbearable headache the first day. Not understanding certain transactions, she was forced to call on John and Ted and Leonard, until they and she were thoroughly annoyed with each other.

"I'm sorry, my head's killing me, but some of these contracts are not filled out. I know I'm crabby, Ted, but you have to keep an accurate account of how things were paid. There's no time in on this contract and it's a billing. I've got to know. And on this other one there's no date out. How am I supposed to bill these people?"

"We were so busy some of the time. I gotta go — there's a customer." And he escaped to the counter.

She longed to return to her bed but instead put her head down on the pile of contracts and took a short nap. The phone awakened her. She jumped and pain stabbed behind her eyes. Would the headaches never cease? She answered when Ted didn't.

It was the insurance company informing her there was a check in the mail. If any of the equipment was found, it now belonged to the insurance company, unless she wanted to buy it back.

She realized she had to make a decision whether to replace the machinery or sell the business. Forgetting the paperwork, she paged through rental magazines, reading business-for-sale ads, knowing she had procrastinated and lost the best selling season. Should she hang on another year, replace some or all of the equipment? Did she have a real choice? Through the glass she saw a customer at the counter. Where the hell were Ted and Leonard?

"Hi, what can I do for you?" She leaned on the counter, squinting at the customer.

"You all right?" he asked.

"Yeah, I'm fine," she lied. "I always look like this."

"I always look like this too." The man laughed. He was filthy, face and hands and clothes smudged with dirt.

She laughed with him. "What have you been doing?"

"Digging. I need a backhoe or a trencher or something to drain off my yard. It's under water. I'm raising mosquitoes and frogs instead of grass and toads."

"A backhoe might be too large a solution to the problem. You want ditches or trenches?"

"A trencher ought to do it."

"Let's look outside and see what's in."

The day was bright with hot sunshine, which gave Amy a worse headache. She leaned against the door frame as she went out the door. The man showed concern.

"Little lady, you lied. You're not all right."

"I was in an accident three weeks ago and my head still hurts."

"Give it time and rest."

"I can't rest any longer. Come on." She started across the lot.

"I'll wait until one of them can help me." The man nodded in Ted and Leonard's direction.

An old truck drove in. "That may be a while. Let's see what we've got and write up the contract."

With a show of reluctance he followed her to the row of trenchers. They had five; three were in. She demonstrated how to operate the Ditch Witch, which she thought rather complicated but he caught on quickly. "How did you find out about us?" she asked. It was a legitimate question because she ought to know which advertising was effective.

"A friend of mine, Dave Bauer, rented a tractor and mower about a month ago, said you saved his life." His smile lit up his eyes.

The man who was run over with a tractor by his son. "I'll never forget. He was generous, to say the least. The wide tire distributing the weight saved him. I was sure something must have been broken."

"He had a few cracked ribs. I'm not just his friend; I'm his doctor."

So that's how he knew something was wrong with her. She felt woozy and grabbed the trencher handlebars.

"I'll take this machine. It's already on the trailer. I can hook it to the car myself. Let's go inside." He took a firm hold of her arm.

Inside the cool building, John was behind the counter signing out a generator. It was a relief to know she could retreat to her office. Covered with sweat, nauseated, vision blurred, she let the doctor lead her to the office.

John drove her home. On the drive he asked if she was planning to replace her wrecked car. "What are you going to buy?"

She had to buy something soon. She had been

taking Deb to work when she needed a car, like today. "I don't know. I haven't even looked. What would you buy?"

"Why not another Grand Am? You got the insurance check, didn't you?"

"Yes, thanks. I have to have the Subaru back before four."

"We'll drop it off," John said curtly. Then: "Maybe you'd better stay home a few days longer."

"I can't, John. I have to catch up on the bookkeeping. We received a check from the insurance company for the stolen equipment." She gently leaned her head against the head rest and closed her eyes.

"Maybe you better call the doctor." He glanced at her, concern on his face.

"I will. I hear you have a girlfriend," she said with a slight smile.

He snorted. "Who told you that?"

"Chris. Marge told her. I hear she's attractive, intelligent and fun. That's nice, John."

"I thought about getting a divorce the other day." He shot a look her way. How would she react? But her eyes were still shut.

"If you want one, get one," she said, betraying no emotion. Expecting John to demand a divorce when she had left him, she had considered then how she would react and thought she wouldn't care. But he had surprised her by saying he didn't want one. Now that she actually tasted rejection, she realized he was her safety net, her security blanket, there if and when she needed someone to fall back on. It was unfair of her to want to hold him for those reasons, yet she did.

"Not now. It would be difficult financially."

So like John to consider finances first, personal happiness second. Well, someone had to be concerned with the family fortunes. He was better at it than she. God, her head throbbed. She felt like she was going to puke any minute and her vision kept going blurry. "When that doctor comes back, the one with the trencher, why don't you ask him how long I'm going to feel this way?"

Inside the apartment the bed rose to meet her and she curled in a ball, her body bathed in sweat. Swallowing rapidly, she forced vomit back down her throat. Maybe she should call school, ask Deb to find another way home. She couldn't bring herself to reach for the phone.

"Well, little lady, you're just going to have to learn to rest."

Struggling out of a bleak dream, one she willingly forgot as soon as she left it, Amy opened her eyes. "What?" The man who had rented the trencher earlier in the day was leaning over her, a friendly smile on his face. She wondered if she was still dreaming, but there was John, looking awkward and uneasy, just behind him. "How'd the trencher work for you?" she asked, rolling onto her back.

Laughing a little, he said, "All business, aren't you? No problems, a good machine. Tell me how you feel."

She told him, glancing from him to John while she talked.

"You're trying to do too much too soon."

"It's been three weeks. I can't stay down any longer."

"Maybe Marge can do the bookkeeping. She hasn't found a job yet," John suggested.

"She's never done it."

"That doesn't mean she can't."

"You can't," the doctor said firmly. "You're to stay in bed another week, at least. Then we'll see."

"What's your name?" Amy asked. She didn't think anyone made house calls anymore.

He reached for her hand. "I'm Brian MacElfresh. Mrs. Netzger, I presume?"

"Amy, call me Amy. All my friends do. Do you make house calls often?"

"Never, this is just a friendly visit. Let me leave my name and number in case you need advice, help, whatever. If you're not better by the end of the week, I want to know."

Reassured and exhausted, she was certain she would now sleep the entire week with a clear conscience. The apartment door closed, and Amy heard it from a great distance as she drifted off. Briefly she wondered how John had gotten into the apartment.

Later, sensing someone, Amy opened her eyes. Deb stood worriedly next to the bed. Amy asked, "Did you have any trouble getting a ride home?"

"Nope. Did you call the doctor?"

"One came to the house. Lie with me a while, will you?"

Deb curled against Amy, napped for fifteen minutes, then got up to fix something for dinner. The phone rang and she snatched it off the receiver.

"Hello." No answering hello, just breathing. "Hello, Deb here."

"Is my mother there?" Marge asked.

"Just a minute, Marge, I'll get her." Anyone outside Amy's family Deb would have turned away, but it wasn't her place to speak for Amy to her family. In the darkened bedroom she gently wakened Amy and handed her the extension. "It's Marge." Deb turned on the light, returned to the kitchen.

"Marge, how are you?"

"Dad said you still have headaches, but I've got to know some things if I'm going to do this bookkeeping."

Feeling better, Amy propped herself up on the pillows. "Like what?"

Fifteen minutes later, Marge said, "I haven't got to the expense book yet. I'll probably have to call you tomorrow."

"Call me any time. I love hearing from you."

"I don't like talking to Deb." Said a little sullenly, a reminder she hadn't forgiven Amy her transgressions.

"I'm glad you're doing the books, Marge, and I understand your not wanting to talk to Deb but she lives here. If you don't want to talk to her, call during school hours."

Deb entered the room shortly after Amy hung up. "Everything okay?"

"I think maybe it will be." Amy smiled, her face pale and pinched as if expecting pain. "Marge is doing the office work since I can't. She had some questions about the books, but she is talking to me again anyway. I don't know how long it'll last."

"It's a step in the right direction."

* * * * *

MacElfresh called at the end of the week. "Amy, how are you? Thought I'd check."

"This isn't Amy, this is her roommate, Deb. I'll get her."

"Just tell me how she is. Did she mention me to you?"

Deb searched her brain for his name. "Are you the doctor who came to the apartment to see her?"

"That's me."

"That was nice. I think she's better. She's sunning on the patio."

"Tell you what, I'm heading out your way. Why don't I stop in?"

"Sure," Deb said with surprise. Was the man after Amy? Did he need patients? She'd never heard of a doctor calling and offering his services free and delivered.

Brian MacElfresh walked around the building to the patio. He wore shorts; his muscular hairy legs hung out beneath them; a polo shirt covered his chest but a chunk of curly hair sprouted at the unbuttoned neck. Grinning, he greeted the women.

"You look different cleaned up," Amy said, shading her eyes. A good looking man, he had a squarish face, dark eyes and hair and mustache, a strong jaw. "Meet my friend, Deb Schmidt."

He and Deb shook hands. "Amy, I thought I'd better check on you. Dave Bauer has been on my case." MacElfresh grinned, displaying long white teeth. "We need to go inside for me to look at you."

Amy gazed into his eyes while he put a light to hers. Deb stood nearby wondering what the hell this man wanted, but she liked him. It was impossible not to.

"Better, much better," he said, straightening. "You can go to work a couple hours a day next week, a little longer if you feel up to it, but don't overdo it or you'll be right back where you were — flat on your back. I'll give Dave a progress report. Now I'm going to play tennis before it gets too hot."

"Nice, isn't he?" Amy asked once he was gone. The man made her feel terrific; his unsought attention to her welfare was both flattering and comforting.

Deb couldn't argue with that; everyone should be so nice. "Do you find him attractive?"

"Don't you?" Amy raised her eyebrows.

"Yeah, he's very good-looking, but I'm not into men."

"Why do you think he's making house calls?"

"Maybe he finds you attractive?"

"I don't think so. I'm not getting those vibes. He's a mystery to me, but I'm changing doctors. To him."

Toward six o'clock, the Escort, towing the trailer with the Zuma strapped on it, pulled into the driveway across the street. Burned from sun and wind, Paula and Jane crossed the street to the patio.

"Why didn't you sail with them today?" Amy asked as Deb watched the two women cross the street.

"Because I wanted to stay with you."

"You two missed a great day," Paula said.

Deb fetched two chairs. "Don't tell us about it."

"I didn't know we were invited," Amy remarked, throwing a puzzled look at Deb.

"I didn't tell you. I didn't think you should go."

"I can make those decisions, Deb."

"Maybe next week," Jane suggested, defusing the conversation.

"I was just worried," Deb apologized.

May stretched toward its end. It had been a lovely month — a warm and enticing preview of summer. Only an occasional headache visited Amy now. Deb would be out of school in a few days, and she had been talking with Jane lately about the fun they would have sailing this summer. Whenever either Jane or Deb brought up sailing, Amy's attention turned to Paula. Was Paula as unhappy about the prospect of Jane and Deb spending the summer sailing together as she was? But what could she say? If she herself could spend the summer sailing, she'd jump at the chance.

Leaning on the counter — Ted was delivering a tractor and Leonard could be heard in the shop sharpening blades on a mower — she stared out the windows at a flawless blue sky. Brian MacElfresh walked through the doors. She never knew who would show up next or what that person would be like. Dealing with the public was not always pleasant but it was seldom dull. She grinned. "Dr. MacElfresh, haven't seen you for a while."

"Thought you got lucky, huh? The name's Brian; my father was Dr. MacElfresh." A tall, tan young man with intense blue eyes — Paul Newman eyes, she thought — accompanied the doctor. "I met your roommate. Now meet mine: Jay Frederick."

Frederick was perhaps the handsomest man Amy

had ever seen. She shook his hand and stared into the blue eyes and grinned. "Hi."

"You're Wonderwoman, right?" Jay asked, smiling at her. "According to Brian here, there's not much you can't do."

Was he mocking her? "You didn't say that, did you?" she asked Brian.

"Isn't it the truth?" Brian raised his hands, palms up.

"God, no. Don't I wish." Her face reddened. "Did you come to introduce Jay and embarrass me or did you need something?"

"I think we need an aerator or something. The ground I trenched is like cement. Grass seed just washes off it."

"Okay, I can fix you up with one."

"Looks like you're feeling pretty good," Brian commented, keen eyes on her face.

"I am, thanks to you. Can I make you my official doctor? I try to do business with people who do business with me."

"Sounds like a satisfactory arrangement, patting each other on the back."

After Brian and Jay drove away with the aerator, Amy went to her office. Why did she feel so rotten? she wondered. Her days were purposeful, her health had returned. Marge had broken her silence, albeit Marge only spoke when necessary. But here she was tied to this place again, and Deb and Jane would soon be spending their days on the Zuma. There was something about their easy camaraderie that so disturbed Amy that she wondered what they were doing when they were together. It occurred to her they might enjoy each other so much Deb would come to prefer Jane's company to Amy's. She knew from experience it was impossible to try to keep two people apart when they wanted to be together. There had been no way John could have kept her away from Deb.

VI

Alan Young knocked on the counter with a filthy fist. "Daydreaming?" he asked. Today he wore no shirt, *sweet* and *sour* were clearly visible tattoos on his dirty sunburned chest.

"Sorry," she replied, not sorry at all. She wished he would go away.

"Got a surprise for you." He grinned at her.

"What?"

"I'll show you."

Following him out in the yard, she recognized the stolen Case backhoe on the trailer behind his battered old truck. "How did you get that?" Suspicion flared anew.

"Picked it up out of a field on the south side. Got a reward on this stuff?"

"Why didn't you just leave it there? The police will want to know where it was. I have to call them." She didn't want to thank him. Why should she? It didn't belong to her anymore. "The insurance company owns it now, not me."

When two policemen arrived, she left them alone with Young. She called the insurance company, who promised to send a representative out the next day. The agent asked her to store the backhoe and whether she had any interest in buying it back. Since she still had the money, she said she would think about it.

Just after she hung up, Brian returned the aerator and invited her and Deb to a party at his place Friday night next. Thanks, she'd be there, she told him, and probably Deb would come too. This was the last week of school. Amy, who had always loved summer, dreaded its coming — Jane and Deb alone — but not enough to ask Deb to work. When she had first asked her to work, she hadn't thought about the ramifications of Deb's appearance at the rental. It might further alienate Chris and David and sweep Marge out of reach.

The police drove off and Young walked to the counter.

"There ain't no reward on that hoe?" he asked.

Meeting his one good eye, Amy lifted her lip in disgust. She was supposed to reward him for returning what he had stolen? Because now she was certain he had taken the equipment. "I don't own it."

"You ain't going to take it back?"

"Depends on its condition. John will have to decide if it's worth the money." Go away, she thought. Don't come back. Rent from Rolly's.

"You ain't going to see the rest of the stuff if you don't offer no reward."

She shrugged. "I've been paid for it."

She was thankful he left then, before she asked him where he had hidden the rest of the machinery.

"What was that all about?" Brian asked.

She told him and relayed her suspicions. "I'm going to sic the insurance company on him."

Brian turned to watch Young drive out of the parking lot in a haze of blue exhaust smoke. "I don't know. He could be dangerous."

The thrill of potential danger swept up Amy's spine leaving goosebumps in its wake.

Chris, home for Memorial Day weekend, bicycled with Marge. It was a struggle to keep her abreast or even in sight, just as it had been running with her. She found it discouraging to have devoted so many hours to exercise and still not be fit enough to catch Marge. But then Marge pedaled like one possessed — head down, body bent over the bars, legs churning. And it was so much hotter here than in Milwaukee. Sweat trickled down her neck and plastered her hair to her head; her legs and arms tingled. She gave up the effort, straightened a little, and began to enjoy the familiar scenery. Summer was already here, the foliage dark and rich, the smell of mown grass strong. Marge's back disappeared over a hill, and Chris felt relief.

But when Marge turned around at the next stop sign to find Chris nowhere in sight, she stopped and waited. She had tied her hair back in a pony tail and she wore a sweat band around her forehead. Annoyed, she watched Chris's leisurely approach and frowned when her sister pulled next to her. "You are so slow, Chris."

"Don't wait for me. I like to look around. I'm going to the rental when I get back. How about you?"

"My help won't be needed with you there."

"It would be nice to work together again. You worked when Mom needed you."

"Not when she was there."

So Chris went without Marge and was glad to see her mother in spite of herself. Thoroughly disapproving when Amy had taken charge of her own happiness, nevertheless Chris understood it more than she admitted. She knew, as Marge and David did, that their father had left Amy alone too much and seemed to need no one.

Most of all, though, there was a bond between Amy and Chris not to be broken. Amy had hauled Chris to all her childhood activities and participated in some way, had supported and encouraged her in every venture, loved her unconditionally — the list was endless. In short, Amy didn't deserve rejection from her children.

Joining Amy behind the counter was as natural as coming home. "Hi, Mom. Busy?"

"Hi, honey, when did you get home?" Strange to have to ask, strange not to be there anymore to greet her children when they returned home.

"Last night. I just went for a bike ride with Marge this morning. I thought I was in shape. She showed me up again."

"You look great, already tan." Amy smiled, thinking Chris always looked terrific, even when she first got out of bed.

"What's going on?"

Amy gave her a rundown on what was out, what was going out, what was expected in. "Where's your dad? I haven't seen him and Grit in a week."

"Out with Marilyn for the day. They're picnicking."

A twinge of irritation plucked at Amy. "Lucky him, not having to work today."

Chris's dark eyes studied her mother. "You can go. I'll stay. Maybe Marge will come in."

"If I weren't here, she probably would," Amy replied without rancor. She wasn't going to crowd Marge. She knew what a mistake that would be. "I wouldn't leave with you here, Chris. It's wonderful to see you."

Marge had finished her ride about the same time Chris had, only Marge had ridden nearly twice as far as her sister. Sweat pouring down her face, she had coasted into the garage, then waited on the porch for Chris to shower. Once out of the shower, the house empty — Grit lay on his side in the front yard, one ear standing straight up, keeping an eye on the property — she put a tape in the tape deck and returned to the porch with a book. It was a good book; she needed a good book to occupy her mind after she wore down her body.

There was no love interest in her life these days. She'd discarded Matthew with ease. Well, not exactly with ease but certainly with a sense of relief. Knowing as soon as it was over that it should never have begun, she no longer trusted her instincts because at first she had thought Matthew wonderful. In the end, he had vanished from her thoughts like yesterday's lunch.

Later she would mow the yard, tend to the flowers, clean house. Doing what she considered her mother's chores or ones she had shared with her mother brought the bitterness back. It seemed unfair for Amy to shrug off her duties, especially when they fell on Marge.

Brian and Jay lived in a renovated two story house in Broad Ripple. "We ought to live around here," Amy remarked as she and Deb searched for the address. "Isn't this where the gay population resides?"

"Not all of us," Deb reminded her. "Is he gay?"

"I'm sure. I met his roommate, this gorgeous guy probably more than ten years younger than he is." Her face broke into a grin as the age difference between Deb and herself came to mind.

Deb reached for her hand and squeezed it. "This must be it. Look at all the cars."

The floors were oak, the walls wainscoted,

making Amy think of wrapping paper. A long hall ran the length of the first floor with a library on one side, a living room on the other, a dining room behind the living room and a kitchen across from that. The rooms were huge and furnished in early-American. An elegant fireplace graced the north wall in the living room, a smaller one was centered on the south wall of the library. And a wonderful screened-in porch extended all across the front of the house.

"Brian, this is just so lovely I don't know how to tell you how lovely it really is," Amy said when she came upon him in the kitchen. The kitchen was lined on three walls with counters and cupboards, a round table stood in the middle on the brick tile floor, plants hung from the ceiling over the kitchen sink in front of a large window.

"I know," Brian admitted with a grin. "I love it. I'm so glad you came and you, too, Deb. Let me introduce you to some of my friends."

Amy had wondered if his friends would all be men, but there were as many women. Now that she was a member of what she considered the gay society she recognized other gay people, whereas before she wouldn't have thought about sexual orientation unless it was flaunted.

"Honey, I tell you it's so hard to get good help, isn't it?"

It was all Amy could do not to laugh. The man who had just said those words was leaning theatrically against the library mantel. She confessed that she managed a business. He operated a gift shop. "Well, my help is pretty good. Not always on time, though, and not always willing to stay late."

"Isn't that the truth? I swear, I have to work late every night because no one else will. Where's your business, honey?" His name was Tim something and he was nearly as beautiful as Jay.

"On the north side. It's a rental business."

"*What* on earth is a rental business? *What* do you rent?"

She laughed; she couldn't help it; but he didn't look like he minded. Perhaps he meant to entertain others. "Everything from chairs to tractors to campers, but not party stuff."

He put his hand on his chest and exclaimed, "Tractors! A little bitty thing like you handles tractors?" Brian walked past and Tim grabbed him. "Do you know what this woman does?"

Grinning at her, Brian said, "I certainly do. That's how I met her." He told Tim about Dave Bauer.

Tim was appropriately aghast and Amy was embarrassed. "What was I supposed to do? Leave him under the tractor?"

Deep in conversation with a woman attorney about women's rights, Deb heard Amy laugh and glanced across the room at her. She heard the woman say, "It's a man's world. It's a constant battle for equal rights."

Deb guessed the woman, Sheila Hargast, to be not much older than herself, probably mid-thirties. "I know I get paid the same salary as men with the same amount of education and tenure," she commented.

"Not enough, right?" Sheila said.

"You're right there."

"If there were more men in the school system,

you'd probably get decent pay. Women are willing to settle for less money than men."

It seemed like such an arbitrary generalization that Deb had to dispute it. "How can you know that?"

Sheila shrugged and lit a cigarette. "I've seen it over and over. Women don't value their services as much as men. It must be the upbringing."

"Don't you get paid as well as the men in your firm?"

Sheila grinned and blew smoke above Deb's head. A woman sat next to her and put an arm around Hargast's waist, a proprietary gesture. "I do but I wouldn't settle for less." She turned and smiled at the woman and placed her arm around the woman's shoulders. "Deb, this is my roommate, Bonnie. Deb teaches high school social studies, Bonnie."

Bonnie looked like her name, Deb thought — bleached hair, pale skin, buxom.

Bonnie said, "I used to teach, ten years of seventh grade history, until I couldn't take the little shits anymore."

"So what do you do now?" Deb asked, truly interested.

"I'm a principal."

She looked about as much like a principal as Deb did a farmer. "Oh," was Deb's comment. "That didn't exactly get you away from the little shits."

"It removed me from the classroom."

Extricating herself from the conversation, Deb found Amy in the kitchen helping Brian.

"What a neat party, huh?" Amy said, putting her arm around Deb, giving her a squeeze and a kiss on the cheek.

"Hey, don't do that in public," Deb protested. Deb lived in fear the school board and authorities would find out she was gay.

"Everyone here is gay, sweetie." Amy patted her lover on the rump and took the hors d'oeuvres plate to the dining room.

After everyone had eaten and there was no food left, miraculously, cigarette paper and little plastic bags of marijuana emerged from purses and pockets. Amy and Deb were seated cross-legged on the floor. "We didn't bring any," Amy whispered to Deb.

"We didn't have any to bring," Deb reminded her.

But there was enough for everyone and neither one of them recalled much of the rest of the evening, except laughing.

It wasn't exactly innocent, Deb knew. With a little encouragement, Jane would make a move on her. The question was did she want it to happen. Deb shook her head. Sure as the world she'd lose Amy. It wouldn't be worth it, and she doubted Jane could make love like Amy. She wondered if anyone could.

Once she had asked Amy where she had learned to make love. Had John taught her? Amy laughed and said she had taught John. And when Deb persisted in asking, Amy answered that she had taught herself by knowing herself. If she knew herself, then it followed she'd know another woman. Deb had to admit it made sense.

A pounding. Deb flung the door open to Jane, who brought the freshness of morning with her.

"Want a cup of coffee before we leave?" Deb asked and poured two cups without waiting for an answer.

"I guess so. It'll make me pee when we're sailing." She sank into one of the chairs at the table.

Deb sat across from her. "Me, too. We can take a dip."

"Something wrong?"

"No, why?"

Jane shrugged. "You look deep in thought."

"How's Paula?"

"Good, fine. How's Amy?"

"Working." Deb looked down at her steaming cup. "So is Paula, of course."

"What does she say about us sailing nearly every day?"

"I don't tell her."

"She doesn't ask?"

"Is it causing problems with you and Amy?" Jane's blue eyes looked innocent.

"Well, she's not real happy about it. Probably because she can't go."

"I don't want to cause trouble between you two."

The hell, Deb thought, smiling crookedly. Deb knew she'd be livid if she were in Amy's shoes, working, while Amy played every day with some other woman — even if the play was innocent. "Forget it." She looked out the patio door at the sunny day, felt a soft breeze drift in and caress them with its warmth. "Let's enjoy the day."

Side by side, they leaned back against the force of wind on sail, heads brushing the water as the boat rushed through it, thighs touching. Had their legs always touched like that or did she just start noticing it? Deb wondered. She edged away a little but the pressure of Jane's leg remained.

Jane turned her head and grinned at Deb, her teeth white, her blue eyes lit with happiness. Then, without a word, she kissed Deb on the mouth.

Startled, Deb pulled back but not before she felt a familiar tingling she recognized. "Don't do that," she said with a frown.

"Why?" Jane asked. "You're very attractive. No one needs to know."

"I would know, and I love Amy."

"I love Paula, but okay, forget it. It won't happen again." However, Jane still grinned.

Deb sat forward and loosed the sheet. The wind dropped as if brakes had been applied. "Let's go in."

"Come on, Deb. I said I won't do it again."

Knowing she should insist on going in, Deb relented. The day was magnificent. Why waste it? The sun, the warm wind, the cool water — she hated to give it up. Annoyed that Jane had made the move, because now she had to do something about it, Deb wished it hadn't happened.

All day she debated the merits of telling Amy. If she did, Amy would probably insist she not be alone with Jane, and Jane would guess she had told. But if she didn't, Amy might guess anyway and if she did find out, she would think Deb was hiding something more. She was thirty-two — did she have to report her activities to anyone? After all, she had done nothing wrong. And the repercussions might fall not just on her and Jane but on Paula, too. How could the four of them continue as friends if she told Amy? At the end of her silent debate, she was still undecided. She would play it by ear. If Amy guessed something was amiss, she would probably confess.

But Amy came home that evening preoccupied. Deb was turning salmon fillets on the grill. An elaborate salad, bright greens and oranges, was on the dining table along with place setting set off by a bouquet of yellow roses. Amy glanced at the table, called a greeting to Deb, and went into the bathroom to shower.

John had asked for a divorce. The cool spray splattered Amy's head and ran down her body. As she fought with her feelings, she scratched at greasy spots on her skin. Reason told her not to feel the way she did, which was abandoned and scared. She pulled shorts and a T-shirt over her still damp body.

Deb found her asleep on their double bed. Alarmed, because sleep did not come easy to Amy and it was unlike her to even lie down after work, Deb lay next to her and kissed her awake. "Are you all right?" Her hands slid under Amy's clothes. "Mmmm," she said with a grin, "no wears."

"Just tired," Amy replied, shifting away a little from the touch.

Did she know what had happened today on the sailboat? Deb wondered. Somehow she was sure Amy must know. Telling Amy with her attentions that the kiss from Jane meant nothing, Deb's mouth closed urgently over Amy's while her hands moved from under the T-shirt to inside the shorts to between Amy's legs. The involuntary gasp her fingers evoked reassured Deb.

"What brought that on?" Amy asked, rolling Deb onto her back.

"The salmon," Deb protested half-heartedly.

"Fuck the salmon," Amy retorted, removing Deb's clothes.

But while they ate, Amy regained some of her powers of perception. "Nice meal, nice roses, nice lovemaking. Why?" She stared inquisitively at Deb.

"Why not?" Deb asked. "Don't I try to have something ready nights when you're working and I'm not?"

"John wants a divorce," Amy said.

"So that's it. You care more than you thought, don't you?" Deb filled a bowl with salad and handed it to Amy. Sometimes she was jealous of Amy's previous life.

Amy said dispiritedly, "I'm on the spot. He wants me to take the rental; he'd pay off the debts. That's supposed to be my settlement. He'd sell the house and we'd split those proceeds."

"Is that fair enough?"

"I don't think so. Even with the debts paid off the insurance business is so much more lucrative. It supported us. Rolly's is putting the rental business under. I want to sell."

"Well, you don't have to agree to his terms, do you?"

"No, I don't think I can." She'd suggested putting the rental business up for sale, splitting the profits if there were any, and he giving her a check from the insurance business every week. He had promised to think about it. But she felt such a malaise about all these developments, she just wanted to sleep.

So Deb didn't confess that night, telling herself Amy shouldn't have to face another unpleasantness.

The truth was, Deb admitted, a new relationship

excited her. Even when denying Jane's intentions, she knew sooner or later they would end up in the sack doing what Amy feared they were already doing.

The next day on the sailboat with Jane the summer sun was intensely hot, the wind light and erratic. As she slid off into the water after Jane, Deb recalled her relief when Amy left too preoccupied that morning to ask what Deb would be doing that day. She felt Jane brush against her, and she swam a little away from the boat.

"Let's put in for lunch," Jane suggested, pushing the craft toward shore.

"Kind of early, isn't it?" Deb inquired lazily, floating on her back studying the puffy white clouds overhead.

"Come on," was Jane's reply as she headed toward an isolated spit of sand. They pulled the hull up on the sand and let down the sail.

Deb hauled out the cooler and set it on the beach. "Are you really hungry?"

"Leave it and come on. I've always wanted to investigate that barn up there." She took a beach towel from the boat.

The barn, shafted with sunlight beaming through broken boards, was cool and deserted. Old hay and straw littered the floor and dust motes danced in the hazy shafts of light. Jane placed the towel carelessly on the straw, then looked directly into Deb's eyes.

A stab of excitement electrified Deb. She ran her tongue nervously over her lips and watched Jane's slow, knowing smile.

"I can't do this," Deb said, recognizing it as a lie.

"You wouldn't be here today if you didn't want

to." She moved close and ran her hands up Deb's rib cage. Then she leaned forward. Their mouths met in a kiss that quickly became urgent.

When they lay apart with flecks of chaff and dust sticking to their naked sweaty bodies, Deb breathed deeply and tried to close her mind to everything but the moment at hand.

Jane rolled toward her and ran a hand over her, then rose on an elbow and kissed her again. The hand became more intimate, rousing Deb to respond in kind. Deb thought fleetingly that this was the way it had been with all her lovers, breathtaking excitement until the novelty was eroded by repetition. She didn't consider why she was doing this or what it might do to her relationship with Amy.

Losing track of time and unable to make it up returning to the launching ramp in the nearly windless afternoon, Deb reached the apartment after eight to find Amy in a furious cleaning frenzy, something she reverted to when under duress.

"Hi. Sorry I'm so late. There was no wind and we were clear across the reservoir." True enough, she thought. She watched Amy dust with a controlled fury that was a little frightening.

"Have a good time?" Amy asked through compressed lips, after a long tense silence. She was at the end of her patience with the sailing duo. She had no experience to deal with what she thought was happening, and she had a vague feeling she deserved unfaithfulness. Had she not cheated on John? But this was agony. She didn't want to think she had put him through this pain. It made her physically ill, tying her intestines in knots, sending her to the bathroom.

"Yeah, it was okay," Deb replied evasively. "There wasn't much wind and it was hotter than hell."

"Tell me about it," Amy said dryly, recalling the heat reflecting in waves off the blacktop in the rental parking lot. Then she turned, eyes blazing, "What's going on, Deb?"

"Nothing. I just like to sail." Deb shrugged. "Want me to vacuum?" she asked, remembering she had vacuumed yesterday.

"Sure," Amy said and returned to dusting.

"Let me take you out to dinner tonight," Deb said later, after shutting off the vacuum cleaner. The apartment was as clean as she'd ever seen it.

"No, thanks. I ate. It's nearly nine. I'm going to bed. It's been a long day." Her face felt stiff. It had been a long, hot, slow day at the rental. She felt it had been wasted.

"Tell me about your day," Deb said, following her into the bedroom.

"There's not enough to tell. No one wants to work in this heat." Amy pulled the covers back, stripped down to T-shirt and panties and lay on the bottom sheet.

Wanting everything to be right with them, Deb sat on the other side of the bed. She lay down and reached for Amy.

"It's too hot, Deb."

"The air's on. It's not too hot in here." But she rolled on her back and let her hands fall to her sides. "You want me to stop sailing?" she asked perversely, knowing she wouldn't.

"As a matter of fact, I do. But I don't want to tell you what to do. Do what you want." She felt their relationship slipping away and didn't know what to do about it.

"Any more on the stolen equipment?" Deb asked.

"Nope. I think I'm going to hang on another winter, though. Maybe advertise then and sell in the spring." Could she get by without buying more equipment? Alan Young had been in again, asking if there was a reward on the stolen stuff. She was thinking about offering a small reward for what she needed in lieu of buying new.

"I thought you couldn't wait to sell," Deb said with surprise. "You were talking about it just last night."

"Changed my mind today. I did want the summer but now it's into it and the best selling time is over. What'll I do anyway?" She didn't need time on her hands if she lost Deb. She turned on her side away from her lover.

Did she know? Deb wondered. The thought of losing Amy hadn't been enough to deter her from seeing Jane. Actually, the realization she might lose Amy only made its impact now as she stared at Amy's back. She felt momentary panic and tentatively touched the turned shoulder. "Would you like a rub?"

"No, I don't think so. I just want to sleep, Deb."

"All right, I can take a hint." Deb went into the kitchen to fix herself a drink and a sandwich. She turned on the television. Occasionally she thought of the afternoon but it seemed a long time ago.

Listening to the sound of the TV, Amy considered what she should ask John for a settlement if she hung onto the rental business until spring. All thoughts of Deb and Jane she pushed aside, and, unable to decide how to divide the marital assets, she slipped into sleep for escape.

VII

"They're getting a divorce. I heard Dad talking to a lawyer on the phone." Another crisis had presented itself to Marge. She feared losing her childhood home, her past wiped out by her parents. She couldn't reproach her dad for his interest in Marilyn. She considered him lucky to have found Marilyn. It was her mother's fault as she saw it and she imparted the news to her brother.

"Well, I don't think we can change anyone's mind," David reasoned. "I wonder how Mom feels about this. I just talked to her and she didn't say anything about it."

"She's the cause of it," Marge responded angrily.

"Don't get on Mom's case, Marge. It's never just one person's fault. You need more interests in your life."

Tears started at the thought of how barren her life had become. She sobbed into the receiver.

"You all right, sis? You want me to come home?" Weeping always alarmed him.

"No, but I think I'll call Chris."

"Tell her hello for me," he said, trying to keep the relief out of his voice. "I'll check in on you tomorrow. Okay?" He didn't really know what to do to comfort his younger sister. He didn't want his parents to divorce either, but he felt helpless to stop it.

Chris wasn't any more sympathetic than David had been. "It was bound to happen," she said matter-of-factly, although she didn't feel that way. She, too, was alarmed. Change in her parents' lives was unwelcome to her. She wanted home where it had always been, but she hid her panic from Marge. "I can't come home right now, Marge. Why don't you visit me this weekend? We'll talk. It's only a five hour drive."

Sniffing back a sob, Marge agreed.

Phoning her father at the insurance agency, Chris confronted him with Marge's suspicions. "Is it true, Dad?"

He sighed. "It's true, hon. We're looking into it. Nothing's been filed yet."

"Why didn't you tell us?"

"We would have. I just said nothing's decided yet, but I did ask your mother for a divorce."

"Does she want one?"

"She agreed to one."

The first thoughts Chris had were where Christmas and Thanksgiving would take place. Why was that so important? They had been special times, though, fun times. "Marge is upset. To be perfectly honest, I'm kind of upset myself."

"I know, hon, I'm sorry."

"Do you know, Dad? You're all caught up in a new life and we're losing the old one." She realized how unfair her accusations sounded. She should be more adult than she felt right now.

"Why don't you come home this weekend?"

"What good would that do? I asked Marge to visit me."

He said, "Good idea. I'll always be here for you, you know."

Chris choked at his words. "I know, Dad. I shouldn't blame you. It just gets to me sometimes." She replaced the receiver, thinking that life sucked.

Marge reached her sister's apartment around nine Friday evening. She had hit the Chicago traffic during rush hour. She stood a little frazzled inside Chris's door. "Nice place, Chris."

"Well, come on in and see it. I'll bet you could use a drink."

"I'd kill for one. Traffic was terrible on the toll road." She followed Chris to her kitchenette. Small but nice was her impression. She watched Chris mix a couple drinks.

"I'll show you the night life. We'll eat out, then take in a few interesting spots." Chris glanced at

Marge, who towered over her. Marge's honey-blonde hair was twisted up off her neck. "I like your hair. It makes you look older, though."

"I want to look older. I like yours, too. Makes you look younger."

Chris's hair hung shoulder length, soft and thick and curling. "I want to look younger," she said with a grin. "But I think I'll put it up tonight. We'll pretend to be sophisticated. 'Course that scares the men."

"I think I scare the men off anyway. Is there something wrong with me, Chris? Seriously." Marge took her glass to the living room and settled on the only chair near sliding glass doors opening to a balcony.

Chris followed her and sank cross-legged on the carpet. She'd always thought Marge beautiful, but there was something standoffish about how she carried herself as if she expected disapproval and was prepared to deal with it. "You're gorgeous. I've told you that before. You don't look soft and pliable, though."

Marge snorted. "You're the one who's beautiful and cuddly-looking."

Chris laughed. "You know I'm not cuddly." She sobered. "You look like you've got your act together."

"I'm getting there. Sometimes I wonder if I'll get to be middle-aged and have nothing and no one."

Chris refrained from smiling. "You don't see what I see when I look at you, do you?"

"Guess not."

"You look like Mom, you know."

"Everybody says so. She's the last person I want to resemble right now."

"She told me not long ago in a letter that she cared very much for Dad but their marriage was lonely for her." Chris studied her bare feet.

"I can't feel for her yet. I know all that, Chris. It just seemed so selfish to leave us and then for a woman . . ." She resisted the urge to throw her glass. It was the first time she had put her thoughts about Amy into words to a family member.

"I think she left for herself and I don't think she thought of it as leaving us. She loves us, you know that."

Marge scoffed, "You call that loving us?"

"You've forgotten all those years she was there for us?" Chris asked softly. "Maybe she decided it was time to do what she wanted to do."

"Live with another woman? You're condoning that?" Marge's eyes blazed fury.

"A little homophobic, aren't you?" Chris raised her eyebrows at her sister and took a long drink.

Marge glanced at her glass and swallowed deeply. "I am. The whole thing infuriates me."

"It did me too at first. How do you know they're doing what you think they are?" She couldn't bring herself to say it aloud, that her mother might be a lesbian.

Marge asked with disbelief, "You think maybe they're not?"

Chris met her sister's eyes. "No, I think it's likely they are, but it's not the end of the world. I'm sure they must love each other." She never thought she'd be saying these words, excusing her mother.

Marge stared at Chris. "Let's not talk about it now. Okay? It makes me want to explode."

"We'll get ready to go out. You want to shower?"

* * * * *

Just like the song that went something like one step forward, two steps back, so her life progressed, Amy thought. She had met Deb, now it appeared she would lose her; her kids stepped toward her, then danced back out of reach; John had let her go and found another woman; he wanted to pay the rental's debts and give it to her while he retained the insurance business.

"I can't do it," she said to him. "It doesn't guarantee enough income. Come spring I want to sell it."

"So what do you want?" he asked.

"Help me sell it." She smiled at him faintly, happy for him despite her growing despair over Deb. "You're going to marry her?"

He met her eyes. A strange, troubled expression crossed his face. "We're going to live together. I'm not going to jump into marriage."

He'd done just that with her, she knew. "I'm glad for you, John."

They were on opposite sides of the counter, and his hands rested lightly on the smooth top. Glancing at them, she could almost feel their rough calluses on her skin, moving gently over her body, scratching it lightly. Deb hardly touched her these days; she was forgetting the feel of Deb's hand, soft and hesitant. She dispelled the sensation with a shake of her head.

"We'll put it together this winter. We can auction the equipment or sell it as a whole, however you want to do it." He leaned on his forearms and his hair fell softly over his forehead.

She resisted the urge to push it back. She didn't want to make false moves of encouragement, although she wasn't certain she had any power over him anymore. "Should I advertise in the rental magazines yet?"

"In a month or two. That's a start. I've given this some thought. Stop paying yourself out of the rental. I'll write you a weekly check and keep you on the insurance."

"How big a check?"

He lifted his shoulders in a shrug. "Two hundred seventy-five?"

It wasn't a whole lot. She hesitated.

"When the business sells, you'll get half, and when the house sells, you'll get half of that. I can't afford any more right now."

"I'll give it a try."

"What'll you do when the business is sold?" John asked.

"I don't know."

"You want to keep operating until it's sold, don't you?"

"Yes." The thought of time on her hands frightened her.

She heard the phone ring while unlocking the apartment door. "Yes?" The apartment was so quiet without Deb. Pain stabbed at her and she pushed it away. She refused to think about Deb and Jane.

"How's my favorite woman?"

"Brian, it's so good to hear your voice." And it was.

"What's new and different? What have you and Deb been up to?"

Without warning she started to cry. She was

doing a lot of that lately, whenever Deb was gone. Disgusted, she told herself enough of that stuff.

"What is it, sweetie?" Brian asked with alarm.

"I don't want to talk about it. It makes me cry. How's Jay?"

"Gone. He was just interested in my money. Get your ass in your car and come on over. I need company for dinner."

Amy started a note to Deb and then decided against it. Let her worry, if she worried at all these days.

In Brian's kitchen, with mellow light illuminating the table and softly falling on the corners of the room, Amy relaxed. "What happened to Jay?" she asked.

"He was just another beautiful boy. It wasn't meant to be," he answered ruefully. "You remember Tim with the gift store at the party? Jay's with him. But what's with you and Deb?"

Amy told him. "She says they're just friends. I don't believe it."

"Why not?" he asked, his voice as quiet as hers.

She shrugged, unable to talk with the tears choking her again.

"What's your sex life like?"

She threw him a despairing look.

He nodded. "I'm sorry," he said, grasping her shoulder.

He confirmed her suspicions with his gentle touch, and she sobbed because there was no sex life anymore.

"Go ahead. Cry. It's good for you. I'll fix you a summer drink that'll knock your socks off. Brian's summer tonic. It's just what you need right now."

She sniffed and wiped her face with a napkin. "Fix me anything, I'll drink it."

"Talk to me, woman."

"I can't stand not knowing, and she won't tell me; she won't talk to me. She says she loves me, that she and Jane are just good friends and she won't give up that friendship. What do you think?"

"I think something's going on sweetie, if the lovemaking is over."

Her heart plunged to her feet. "It eats at me; it's a physical thing. I can't seem to let her go."

Brian sat across from her and pointed at her untouched drink. "Drink it," he ordered. "I want another one."

She drank but hardly tasted it. "Did this ever happen to you, Brian?"

"More times than I care to remember," he admitted, taking their glasses to the counter for a refill. "You think I trust those gorgeous young men?"

"Why don't you try for someone older and more stable?" she asked.

"I have. That really hurts when it fails."

"And you think my relationship with Deb is failing?"

"I think you should be more assertive. Maybe ask her to move out, tell her you can't live like you are. Obviously it's tearing you apart."

"I think that would be worse," Amy said in a whisper, imagining not seeing Deb at all. "I'm crazy about her for some reason." She drank absently. Her head started to float away from her. "What's in this?" she asked, holding the glass up.

"Let's eat," he said. "I don't want you off in never-never land before I get my two words in."

During dinner he amused her with a monologue about life with Jay, and she laughed until her jaws ached. It was all new to her, this life. She didn't know what to expect out of a gay relationship, and she asked him.

"Loyalty, friendship, love," he replied, twisting her heart with his words.

"I better call Deb," she said, frowning at the clock.

"Tell her you're spending the night," he called after her. "You're not fit to drive home."

But there was no answer. Ten o'clock and Deb wasn't home. She sighed and carefully made her way back to her chair, bumping into the corner of the table on the way. They finished off the dinner wine.

The next morning she couldn't figure out where she was. If this wasn't her place, and obviously it wasn't, then whose was it and where was the john? When she stood, a ball inside her head crashed against the walls. Reeling to the door and down the hall to an equally strange bathroom, she recalled where she was: Brian's house. She washed her face with cold water, staggered back to the bedroom, and gently lowered herself to the bed. When she woke next, the bedside clock read eleven-ten and thirst drove her back to the bathroom.

Brian woke her around twelve-thirty. "What kind of company are you? Get your ass out of that bed."

"What kind of host are you?" she shot back. Her tongue had grown fur on it.

"Look at this gorgeous day, and you want to sleep it away."

In the kitchen, she remembered Deb. "I better call Deb. She'll be pissed."

Deb had spent the night wondering if she should call John or the police and had done neither. "Where the hell are you?"

"I tried to call you around ten last night. You weren't home," Amy countered.

"I was out for something to eat. I was worried out of my head."

"I'm at Brian's. Had dinner here last night and too much to drink."

"It's okay to scare the hell out of me?"

"I'm not going to argue over the phone."

"I'll see you later."

"Well?" Brian asked when Amy returned to the kitchen.

"You know, Brian, I'm too old for this shit," Amy said.

"You gambled. That was brave of you."

She snorted. "Most people would think I was stupid."

"Are you sorry?" he asked.

"No. I can't tell you why, though."

"Let's go to the feminist bookstore," he suggested. "It's right up the street. There's someone I want you to meet."

Looking around the shop with interest, curiously eyeing the women studying the merchandise, Amy wandered among the shelves, while Brian talked to the woman behind the counter. He called to Amy.

"Kelly Barnard, Amy Netzger. Kelly runs the store, Amy."

The two women shook hands. "Interesting place," Amy commented.

Brian grinned at her. "You've never been here, have you?"

"No," Amy admitted. "I didn't know this place existed."

Amy sized up the other woman. Forties, hair short and wavy, the brown peppered with gray, eyes dark and friendly behind wire-rimmed glasses; she was a couple inches taller than Amy and heavier. Intelligent, comfortable to be with, fun — probably all those things, Amy speculated.

Brian pointed to the notices on the wall next to the stairs. "You ought to consider going to some of these meetings," he said to Amy.

Flushing, she read a few of the fliers. "Sheila Hargast is speaking?" she asked Kelly.

"Next Thursday, in fact," Kelly said. "Why don't you come? We have a meeting every Thursday anyway and just talk among ourselves if there's no speaker. It's always fun."

"I won't know anyone," Amy said, more to herself than to the others.

"Well, I'd come but men aren't all that welcome," Brian said.

"You'll know me," Kelly said. "Everyone's very friendly. Be my guest."

"I will. I'd like that."

"You're going to stay for dinner, aren't you? Might as well now you're here. You don't come that often."

Deb and her mother were standing in the entryway of the ranch house where Deb had spent her youth. Her mother moved back into the living room, and Deb walked past her into the familiarity of her youth. Memories always assailed her when she returned to this house. Her past wrapped itself around her like a blanket.

Her mother's back appeared to have broadened. It was straight as a board, as it had always been. Mary Schmidt was in her late fifties, with almost no gray hair among the dark. Her eyes, large and hazel, gave the appearance of being startled. She poured coffee and sat across the table from Deb.

"How are you, Ma? You look terrific."

"I was out last night with Stan. We went dancing."

Stan Stepanek lived across the street. He had to be nearly ten years older than her mother — a big man with snow white hair and a ready grin. Somehow she couldn't picture her mother dancing. "That's nice."

"He's a nice man. He wants to marry me."

Startled, Deb stared at her mother with interest. "Well? Are you thinking about it?"

Mrs. Schmidt spooned sugar into her cup and poured milk over it. "Now and then. I like things the way they are, though. You know how men are."

As a matter of fact, Deb felt like saying, I *don't* know how men are. Her father had died when she was seventeen. She remembered him as a quiet, undemonstrative man — a stranger. "How are they?" she asked out of curiosity.

Mary set her spoon down next to her cup and

considered her daughter. "I guess you wouldn't know, would you now?"

Thinking she should have avoided this subject, Deb shook her head while returning the steady gaze.

"They're bossy, even the best of them. I don't think they can help it. I kind of enjoy being my own boss."

Deb howled with laughter. "Mom, I'll bet there's not a man alive who can boss you around."

Mary grinned, took a sip of coffee, and set the cup down with a decisive clank. "I been wanting to ask you something."

For a second everything stopped functioning, then picked up speed. She knew her mother was about to ask.

"You know, you didn't date much, you always had lots of girlfriends. Are you, you know, one of them who like women more than men?"

A major breakthrough, Deb thought. Sex was not one of her mother's normal topics of conversation. What to say? A smile stole across her face. "Does it really matter, Mom?" she asked, meeting her mother's eyes. She shrugged. Her heart was in her throat, beating so loudly she could hear it.

Mrs. Schmidt sighed and made a face. "What did I do wrong?"

"Nothing, Mom. I don't think there's anything wrong with me. I just prefer women to men. They're more sensitive, more affectionate . . ."

"How would you know?" her mother broke in.

The two women looked at each other. "I guess I don't know. But it's nothing you did, Mom. I've been this way as long as I can recall." At least she didn't have to hide it anymore from her mother. Maybe they could finally be friends.

"You live that way with Amy?"

Of course it was the logical progression of thought. "I care very much for Amy."

Mrs. Schmidt stoically studied her coffee. Deb hesitantly touched her mother's hand.

"Ma, I did try to be straight, I really did. Remember, I went with George Shelpman in high school?" She frowned as she thought of Shelpman, a beefy, florid football player.

"A nice boy," her mother said, brightening.

"Nice boy, my ass. His hands were always where they didn't belong."

"Oh. Well, that's the way men are." Said with a shrug.

"Shit," was Deb's comment.

Deb's mother leaped to her feet in an explosion of energy and bustled around the kitchen.

"Relax, Mom. I'd like to talk to you. It's nice to be able to talk to you. It's good not to have to hide everything from you."

"You mean it's nice not to lie to me anymore." The older woman took a large bowl out of the refrigerator.

"When you're gay you spend your days lying to people. You have to."

"I hate that word," her mother muttered.

"What word?"

"It's supposed to mean happy. Queer's better." Her voice shook.

Had her mother slapped her, Deb would have felt less hurt. Give her time, she told herself.

"I put a roast in a while ago," Mary said after five minutes of no conversation.

"I can smell it," Deb grunted. "It's making me hungry."

"You can break beans to go with it."

Deb loved green beans the way her mother prepared them. "Sure," she said enthusiastically. "Tell me about Stan."

"Want I should invite him to dinner too?"

"Why not? The more the better."

"You won't say anything about what we were talking about?"

"Oh, Mom, it's taken years for me to tell you. You think I'd tell someone I don't even know?"

Mary Schmidt heaved a ponderous sigh. Considering that parents took admissions of homosexuality by their children as personal failures in parenting and reacted accordingly, Deb was amazed her mother was holding up as well as she was.

After dinner, driving home, Deb leaned back against the headrest, more relaxed than she'd been in weeks and closer to her mother than she ever thought she'd be.

That evening the sun set the western sky aflame. Sitting on the patio in the growing dark, the radio playing in the living room behind her, Deb contemplated life without Amy. She sipped at a vodka and tonic and wondered how she could have risked losing Amy. If Amy walked through the door right now, she'd take her in her arms.

Around midnight Amy let herself into the darkened apartment. Tiptoeing down the carpeted hallway, she started at the sound of Deb's voice. Deb lay on their bed.

"Where you been, Amy?" Her voice slurred the words. "Would have been thoughtful to call."

"I did. You weren't here. Sailing with Jane, I suppose?"

"No. Spent the day at my mother's." Deb raised herself on an elbow and peered at Amy. "Come here."

"You're three sheets to the wind," Amy said, going into the bathroom.

Deb got to her feet and followed Amy. "It's lonesome here without you, you know that?" Bracing against the wall, she saw herself in the mirror. She ran her fingers through her hair and over her face. Why the hell had she drunk so much?

Amy snorted, watching Deb in the mirror. "Tell me about it," she said sarcastically. "I'm an expert on what it's like to be here alone."

Deb staggered back to the bed and fell on it. She'd have to sleep this off. "We'll talk tomorrow," she said and floated into unconsciousness in a dizzy wave.

VIII

Rain had fallen — three inches in an hour — accompanied by high winds. Basements flooded, trees and limbs fell indiscriminately. A representative from the fire department woke Amy at five Thursday morning, when the storm abated, and she opened the rental to supply the city with pumps and chainsaws. She stayed at the store and worked on the books until opening time, when customers lined up for the remaining chainsaws and pumps. All the loader tractors, the two cherry pickers, and the extension ladders were rented by nine a.m. When it came time to close, she was exhausted, physically and otherwise. The last thing she wanted was to go out that night.

If Deb had been home when she returned Thursday evening, Amy probably would have stayed, but Deb's absence gave her the impetus to go to the meeting at the feminist bookstore. But where could Deb be? Overcast and cool, the day was not one to sail. By the time she locked the door behind her, despair gnawed at her again like something alive.

The streets and nearby parking lots overflowed with vehicles. Amy was forced to park a few blocks away from the bookstore. Hesitating because of the crowds outside, Amy paused on the sidewalk and took a deep breath. She saw no one she knew at first and was so engrossed in perusing the crowd, she jumped when someone touched her arm.

"You look so familiar. Haven't I met you before?"

Amy turned. "Bonnie, isn't it?" she asked, eyeing the bleached blonde hair.

"Yeah. Amy, right? We met at a party at Brian's."

Relieved not to be alone among all these strange women, Amy stopped searching for Kelly until Kelly stood in her line of vision.

"I've been looking for you everywhere. I thought maybe you weren't here."

"Kelly Barnard, this is Sheila Hargast's roommate, Bonnie. Bonnie's a school principal."

"I keep the little shits in line," Bonnie said mildly.

"The little shits, huh," Kelly commented, laughing. "Come on, let's go upstairs."

After Sheila spoke, groups of talking women

formed and re-formed like a kaleidoscope. Listening, Amy circulated from group to group until Kelly caught up with her again.

Amy realized she really liked this woman, but then she remembered she had liked Jane at first, too. Maybe she wasn't such a good judge of character.

"Will you stay a while," Kelly asked.

She shouldn't encourage this woman, she knew, but she was so starved for company. "I'm the boss, which should mean I can sleep in tomorrow but what it really means is I have to be there. But I'll stay." She shrugged. She'd probably be worthless tomorrow, but what the hell.

When it got to be midnight, she told Kelly she had to leave. "I wish I could stay longer."

"May I call you?"

Amy didn't even hesitate. "That would be nice." They exchanged numbers.

So many things had changed for Deb with the start of school. The only days she was now free were weekends, and then, of course, Paula was home and she was uncomfortable around Paula. Even though Jane still asked her to sail with them, she found excuses not to go. Saturdays were loose-end days, when she caught up with class work or cleaned the apartment or shopped or visited friends.

The second Saturday of September, as she drove along Broad Ripple Avenue, she spotted Amy seated outside a restaurant with another woman. Deb came close to colliding with the car in front of her. She parked and walked back to the corner. No doubt that it was Amy, talking animatedly with this other woman.

Should she confront them? She had no right. Perhaps it was just a friend. But Amy had said she would be working today and Deb knew all of Amy's friends. Jealousy gripped her with surprising strength. She walked back to the car.

Amy and Kelly were just finishing lunch. It wasn't the first time they had been together; they had spent a few afternoons in each other's company when Amy had been able to break free from the rental.

"I'd like to spend tomorrow with you," Kelly said.

Amy hesitated. Deb would be home tomorrow. She'd probably want to do something, but she hadn't suggested anything yet. Amy decided not to try to hide Deb anymore. "I don't know. You know I live with someone, don't you?"

Kelly's eyebrows shot up. She smiled, her dark eyes large and luminous behind the lenses. "I thought you might."

"I should have told you."

"I'd like to be friends anyway."

"Oh, so would I," Amy replied and her voice dropped a decibel. "Deb and I have a few problems right now."

"I don't want to be one of them," Kelly remarked dryly. She ran one hand through her hair and it sprang back in unruly waves.

Amy met her eyes. "Actually, we have more than a few problems. There might be nothing left to salvage."

"You still care?"

Amy nodded and looked at her coffee. "I do but I don't think she does."

Kelly leaned forward, resting full breasts on crossed forearms. "Forget tomorrow, but when you want to talk to someone, call me. I know what it's like to lose someone you love. It's one of the hardest things to get through. But, and this is a big but, I'll never interfere in another relationship. It happened to me, I'll never do it to someone else." She patted Amy's arm. "Think of me as a friend. Make sure your roommate knows I'm just a friend, too."

Amy nodded and smiled sadly.

"Don't throw me in her face," Kelly added with a rueful grin.

Amy laughed. She had been tempted to do just that. "I won't."

She didn't have to. Deb confronted her shortly after she arrived home that evening. "I thought you had to work today."

"I did," Amy said as she headed toward the shower.

Deb followed, and sat on the toilet lid. "I saw you in Broad Ripple this afternoon with another woman."

Amy bridled at the injustice of it, the nerve. "I had lunch with a friend. So what?"

"I don't know that woman."

"If you had been around more, you would have met her. She called me at work."

"Who is she?"

Amy turned on the shower and stepped in, pulling the curtain shut behind her. "Her name is Kelly Barnard. She runs a feminist bookstore."

"How did you meet her?"

"What is this third degree?"

"Tell me. Please."

"Brian introduced me to her and I went to a meeting at the bookstore one night when you were out with Jane somewhere."

"You never told me."

"Why should I? I don't know what you do when you're not with me."

"If that's the way you want it . . ." Deb started out the door, then stopped. "Are you sleeping with her?"

Silence, except for the sound of water falling.

"Did you hear?"

"Wait until I get out."

Deb sat back down. Amy turned off the shower and stepped out.

"Now, did you ask what I thought you asked?" Her voice was controlled fury.

"Are you sleeping with her?" Deb repeated the question.

"You have no right to even ask. Aren't you sleeping with Jane?"

"No." She hadn't slept with Jane in weeks.

"You were, though, weren't you?"

Deb saw the anger in Amy's eyes. "You are sleeping with her, aren't you?" She had to know.

"God, you have a lot of nerve," Amy said, drying herself, her voice shaking.

"You're denying it?"

"There's nothing to deny. We're friends is all. Jesus, I can't believe this."

"I was jealous when I saw you with her today." Deb spoke quietly, seriously. "Amy, can we talk?"

"I'm tired. I'm hungry." She met Deb's troubled

eyes and capitulated. "Sure. Is there anything to eat?"

In the kitchen, Deb handed Amy a drink. "Tell me about her."

"First you tell me what went on this summer," Amy countered, "and why it's over, if it is."

Deb glanced at Amy, who was dressed in old sweats, her hair dripping. "You really want to know?"

Amy nodded. She believed she could handle it now that she had Brian and Kelly for backup. "I've got to know, if we're going to get on with our lives."

"It'll mean trouble for me," Deb said.

"I can't make trouble for you if you no longer care," Amy replied.

"You've got to know I care. I wouldn't be jealous if I didn't."

"Some people hate to lose any possessions."

Astonished, Deb said, "I've always cared, Amy. I love you. It's just that it was so exciting. You know?"

Well aware of how it could be, Amy replied, "I know how it is. So you were intimate with her."

Looking blindly at the salad she was creating, Deb replied softly, "Yes, at one time I was."

"And you wouldn't tell me. You let me wonder and worry. It actually made me sick to think about the two of you." Undirected fury raged in Amy.

"I'm sorry. I didn't want to lose you."

"Well, you just did." Amy threw the onion in the salad, scattering lettuce all over the counter.

"Goddamn it, that's not fair, Amy. You ask me to be honest, then you use it against me." She grabbed

Amy, who had started out the room, and pushed her against the counter. "Listen to me."

"How dare you shove me around," Amy sputtered.

"You move and I'll sit on you," Deb threatened, afraid to let Amy out of her sight for fear she'd keep going and Deb would never see her again.

A wild laugh started up Amy's throat, and she swallowed it. "Talk then." She crossed her arms and glared.

Deb slumped. What was there to say? "I don't really have an excuse. I never initiated it," she said, knowing she'd probably do it again if the circumstances were the same. "I couldn't resist is all. It's over, though. See, I thought I could handle both of you, and I couldn't. After a few weeks, I didn't want anybody anymore."

Amy turned away and leaned against the counter, her fists clenched. She felt physically ill. Through the anger, the hurt, the frustration, she understood in spite of herself. She admitted in a soft voice, "I know. I don't want anyone either. You don't need to worry about Kelly, not yet anyway."

Jealousy reasserted itself in Deb. Hesitantly, shyly, she reached for Amy. "I miss you."

Amy moved abruptly away from Deb's touch. "You tell me you screwed someone else and in the next breath you say you miss me," she said with renewed anger. "I just want to go to sleep. Alone," she added pointedly.

"Eat something first," Deb urged, saying the first thing that came to mind, anything to keep communication open between them.

"Stuff it."

Deb dumped the salad makings in the garbage

and slammed out of the apartment. Day faded early into night now that it was mid-September, and fall chilled the air. Wishing she had grabbed a jacket but unwilling to go back for one, she walked for blocks until her legs numbed with exhaustion.

Sleeping apart in the apartment where they had always slept together kept Deb awake most of the night. Several times she rose and looked into Amy's room, annoyed at Amy's ability to sleep through this crisis. For such a long time it had been Amy who had difficulty falling asleep and Deb who had drifted off as soon as her head hit the pillow. Fortunately, tomorrow was Sunday; Deb wouldn't have to teach. She stood uncertainly in Amy's doorway and wondered what Amy would do if she crawled into bed with her and held her. Instead she returned to her solitary bed and fell into a restless sleep.

IX

Brian opened the door wide and swept an arm across the threshold. "Want a drink or something? Then we'll take a walk to the Greek place for dinner."

Brian and Deb sauntered through the September twilight in silent camaraderie, enjoying the mellow light and soft breeze. "Makes you want to sing, doesn't it?" Brian observed.

"It's lovely out, yes." But the truth was, when she felt shitty that was all she could think about.

When they spied Amy and Kelly at a table

outside the Mexican restaurant, Deb said, "I don't want her to see me," and, ready to run, backed toward the corner. "You introduced her to that woman?"

"Afraid I did. She's a marvelous woman."

"Just what I want to hear, Brian," Deb remarked.

"We'll go around the block here and slip into the Forum."

Ordering a kir, Deb swished the liquid around in the glass. She felt Brian's eyes on her and met his gaze.

He grinned wryly. "To friends and lovers." He raised his glass to hers.

Deb laughed. "Is it too late?" she asked, serious again.

"I don't know, Deb. I don't think so. You hurt her pretty bad, though."

"I know. I don't know what got into me. For some reason I had to do what I did. I never knew what it would be like to lose her. Got any ideas on how to get back into her good graces?"

"You know her better than I do." He shrugged. "Love her. Are you all through with that other woman?"

"We're still friends."

"I don't know how she's going to like that," he said.

Deb's jaw set.

Amy and Kelly walked back to Kelly's apartment and settled in chairs on the balcony overlooking the swimming pool. Amy was satisfied just taking comfort in the other woman's company. She forgot Deb and the surge of pain Deb's infidelity had caused. When she felt Kelly's hand on her leg, she turned toward her, surprised, yet knowing she shouldn't be surprised, even though Kelly had said just yesterday she'd never interfere in another relationship. Amy glanced at the hand on her thigh and back at Kelly. What to say?

"I'm here for you," Kelly said in a low voice.

"That's nice to know," Amy replied.

Kelly removed her hand, and her teeth gleamed white in the dark. "You mean a lot to me, Amy."

What was wrong with a friendly fuck? Amy thought. But that was the problem. Sex was just too personal; it led to so many complications, none of which she was sure she could handle right now. Better to say no and stifle those stirrings — she couldn't deny she felt desire.

Home just after Amy, Deb walked down the hall and leaned against the door frame of Amy's bedroom. "I missed you today," she said.

Throwing her clothes over a chair, Amy replied, "I missed you too. Sorry I got so pissed last night when you finally told me the truth." But she started feeling angry again as she said the words.

Deb moved to stand in front of Amy and ran her hands up Amy's arms.

Amy backed way. "No, Deb, not now."

"You were with that woman again," Deb stated flatly, her arms falling to her sides.

"Yes, I was. I like her. She's interesting."

"Great. I just wish none of this had ever happened." Her voice registered defeat.

"So do I, Deb, but it did."

"Can't we put it behind us?"

"Maybe, but not yet."

"I don't know if I can live like this."

"I lived this way all summer, not knowing what was going on, certain something was going on. You don't have to live like this." The spurt of indignation died.

"What does that mean?" Deb asked, sitting on the end of Amy's bed.

"It means you don't have to live here if you don't want to." It was anger talking. It wasn't what Amy wanted. If she could have erased the summer, she would have.

"You want me to leave? Is that what you want?"

"No, it's not what I want." Amy sat cross-legged on the bed.

"I want you," Deb said suddenly and moved toward Amy again.

"Don't," Amy warned, her legs suddenly weak, a sure sign of excitement.

With sudden strength Deb shoved her back on the bed and held her down. "Don't tell me you don't want me." She moved to kiss Amy, but Amy turned her head away. Deb's free hand caressed her and slid into her underpants. "You do want it," she said knowingly, her fingers in the warm wetness.

Refusing to look at Deb, knowing how much she did want her and yet too angry to admit it, Amy said in a dangerous whisper, "Are you going to force me, Deb?"

Deb gave an abrupt laugh, withdrew her hand and released her. "You're playing games," she stated flatly, sitting up on the edge of the bed.

Incensed, Amy rose on an elbow. "You're the one who plays games."

"Yeah, maybe I do. I admit it, though. See you tomorrow."

The kids gathered in Deb's room — laughing, talking, pushing. They needed her easy acceptance; she needed the diversion they offered. Sitting behind her desk, leaning back in her chair, listening to the girl perched on the corner of the desk, she pushed away the tiredness. Never had she felt so tired.

"I wish you'd coach volleyball, Miss Schmidt. Miss Vanderhayden's not much fun, and she don't coach the way you do."

"Doesn't, she doesn't coach," Deb corrected without thinking. "I had volleyball for years, kiddo. I begged out of it last year."

"Won't you take it back? Please," another girl pleaded.

Deb gave a soft, pleased laugh and thought that if she were still coaching she wouldn't get home before Amy did. "Tell you what. I'll help with the floats instead."

"Will you chaperone the dance Friday night?" one of the other girls asked, interrupting the political argument she was conducting with another boy.

"Who are you going to vote for?" the boy wanted to know.

Deb raised her hands, palms toward the students. "Hold it. One question at a time. Yes, I'll be at the dance. And I never tell who I'm going to vote for. I don't want to influence anyone." What a laugh, she thought. She had an impact on her students. Her intention was to make them think, open their minds beyond their parents, and she thought she succeeded admirably.

As she headed for the typing room, the thought came to her that if she did her class preparations at school, she could avoid the apartment until Amy got home. Maybe tonight something could be worked out between them. Something had to be resolved so she could sleep again. Her entire body sagged, and her legs felt as if they weighed one hundred pounds apiece.

When someone knocked on the door, she pulled her mind out of the test she was making up and was astonished to see Jane peering through the door window. Deb waved her into the room. "What brings you here and how did you find me?" She frowned at Jane, both glad and worried to see her. If Amy knew they saw each other, it would probably drive her further away and closer to Kelly.

Jane's eyebrows arched. "Not glad to see me?"

"I'd like to be friends."

A smile twitched at the corners of Jane's mouth and grew into a grin. "Whatever," she said. "I miss talking to you. You know, we're both teachers. There's always a lot to talk about. Can you go out to eat tonight?"

Why not? But Amy would probably call Kelly if Deb didn't go home, and that was enough to make her want to go home. "I don't know. What about Paula?"

"Paula has something going on tonight, and I'd like to eat at Olive Gardens."

"I love eating there. I'll call Amy and tell her I'll be late."

Amy sounded distant on the phone. "You don't have to call, Deb. You didn't last summer."

"Goddamn it, Amy, how could I call from the reservoir?" she hissed into the phone, hoping no one heard her. "I don't want to fight about that anymore. It's over."

"Who are you going to dinner with?" Amy asked.

Deb hesitated. "One of the other teachers."

"Have fun. I'll be late tonight anyway. I have to go to the bookstore after work. I promised I'd help Kelly with a load of books."

Tit for tat, Deb thought, but she felt sick inside when she hung up. She'd forego seeing Jane again if she thought Amy would do the same with Kelly, but she couldn't ask that. Or could she?

"How is Amy?" Jane asked, as they walked toward the room with the copy machine.

"Busy but otherwise okay." Too bad the four of them couldn't be friends any longer, Deb thought.

Sitting on the floor unboxing books, Amy read excerpts from the more interesting looking ones. "I never knew there were so many books like this," she said to Kelly, who stood on a short ladder rearranging shelves.

"Like what?" Kelly asked, pushing her glasses back up her nose.

"Like these." Looking for prurient passages, Amy paged through a novel.

"You mean gay books, lesbian books, as opposed to straight books?"

"Yeah. It's real interesting."

"Think so, huh?" She climbed down the ladder and stepped over boxes to stand behind Amy. "Hmmm, that's pretty hot," she remarked, reading the pages Amy had found. "We have videos too. Would you like to see one?"

Amy laughed to cover her embarrassment. "I'd like to take one home."

"Why don't we watch one sometime. Some are very good — tasteful, I mean."

"Sure." Where was this leading? Where Jane and Deb had gone this past summer? Was she getting even? If so, Kelly was too good a woman to use for that purpose.

"I never did tell you about Deb, did I?" Amy asked.

"No, you didn't."

"Maybe I should. I like you, Kelly. I do and I'm real vulnerable right now."

Kelly sat on the ladder, chin in hands. "I'm listening," she said.

As she talked, one part of her stood off and listened. She sounded a fool in her own ears. First she had let go of a stable relationship with John and had risked losing her children. Now she was unable to give up Deb even when Deb cheated on her. "I am a fool," she said abruptly. "I'm crazy about this woman in spite of everything, and yet I can't forgive her. I want to forgive her, and then I look at her and I get so angry. God, I miss her. I miss talking to her, I miss her in bed, I miss doing things with her. But I can't look at her without getting mad."

She wondered if Kelly made sense of her words. "You said you knew what it was like to lose someone you loved to someone else." She looked at Kelly, who nodded. "Then you know what it feels like when someone you love so much makes love with someone else. You know what they're doing. You can see them in bed together. I can't even think about it. It drives me insane. I'd like to kill Jane, and yet I know it's not her fault alone." Realizing her words might hurt Kelly, Amy stopped. But better to hurt her now than let her think Deb could be brushed off.

"Well, it's obvious you still love her and she says she loves you. Talk to each other."

Amy couldn't read Kelly's expression. "I wish I didn't love her," she said dejectedly.

"But you do," Kelly remarked, "and I'm glad you were honest with me, because I'm very attracted to you."

"Talking isn't easy when I'm so angry. We end up fighting."

"It's the only way you'll work it out. You have to want it bad enough to swallow your pride."

"I know."

She resolved to discuss her differences with Deb that very evening. But then she followed the Subaru and Camaro down the street and surmised that Jane was the other teacher with whom Deb had had dinner. She and Deb got out of their cars at the same time.

"How's that for timing?" Deb said nervously, realizing Amy now knew she had been with Jane.

"Have a nice dinner?" Amy asked coldly.

"Jane and I are just friends, Amy."

"It doesn't matter, Deb." But it did matter. The rush of anger, when she knew Deb had been with Jane, and the feeling of betrayal made her aware of the hope she had harbored that their relationship might be saved.

Deb reverted to a defensive position. "I knew this would happen. That's why I said I was going out with another teacher."

"I told you it doesn't matter. Go out with whoever you want." Amy went down the hall to the bathroom to get ready for bed. Maybe she had been stupid to tell Kelly how much she still cared for Deb, but the thought of starting a new relationship with someone else didn't appeal to her. She wanted to crawl into bed and lose herself in sleep.

"We've got to talk," Deb said from the doorway.

"Why? What's to talk about?" Amy threw her clothes in the hamper and turned on the shower.

"Everything." Deb undressed and followed Amy into the shower. She grinned at the surprised look on Amy's face. "We used to do this every day."

"Can't you wait until I'm done?" Amy scowled.

"No, I can't. Look at me, Amy. What do you see?"

"A naked woman," Amy said, shampooing her hair.

"Let me do that for you."

"I can do it. You want to get under the water?"

"That would be nice."

Amy had shut her eyes against the soap and water on her face.

Impulsively, Deb put her arms around Amy and pulled her close. It was like coming home.

Stiffening at the unexpected touch, then responding to the silky softness of Deb's body against her own, Amy found herself automatically embracing the other woman. Deb's mouth moved up Amy's neck, reached her cheek, and then softly sought her lips. It had been such a long time for Amy who had been celibate except for occasional lapses when her own hand relieved her physical needs.

There was urgency to complete the act: Deb afraid Amy might push her away, Amy fearing Deb might change her mind. They fell on the bed in a tangle of limbs.

After the first frantic satisfaction, Amy covered Deb with her body, then began a slow descent — tasting, kissing, touching as she worked her way to the joining of Deb's legs, where she buried her face in the mound of wiry black hair.

Deb's hips rose. Her hands gripped Amy's hair. She heard herself moan as she began to move toward that center of excitement, faster and faster, until it exploded and released her.

Working her way back up Deb's body and enfolding her in her arms, Amy listened to Deb's breathing, to the pounding of her heart. She loved the feel of their bodies together — the softness of breasts, the smoothness of skin — even now when they were wet with sweat.

Amy closed her eyes to feel better the gentle sensation of Deb's mouth and hands as they moved from her face to her neck to her breasts and on down her body. She arched her back and gasped at the expected touch of tongue.

When it was over, Deb held Amy tightly and whispered contentedly, "We're going to need another shower." She felt Amy nod. "You know what I felt like when I took you in my arms in the shower?"

"What?" Amy asked, languid with sexual satisfaction.

"It was right, it was natural, we belonged together, holding each other."

Amy's hands began to move again. "I don't think I can get enough of you."

Deb spoke without thought. "I never felt this way with Jane."

Amy rolled on her back away from Deb. "I don't want to hear how it was with you and Jane — ever."

"Jane is just a friend."

"You sleep with all your friends?" Amy showed her back to Deb.

"Don't," Deb said, turning Amy toward her to hold her again. "We won't talk about it."

They took another shower together, drank some wine while sitting in bed, and talked — reluctant to lose each other in sleep.

That night Deb slept soundly for the first time in weeks. Curled against her, Amy replayed the evening in her mind until exhaustion stilled her thoughts.

X

Saturday morning Deb and Amy loaded their bikes on the rack on top of Amy's car and drove to Brown County State Park, where the Indianapolis Bike Club members were to meet. Amy had joined the club one lonely evening in August. She had talked to a few members that first night and one of the people who had greeted her had been Marilyn, but, of course, she hadn't known Marilyn was connected with John.

At least fifty people showed up at the designated

parking lot. Deb and Amy were among the first and drank McDonald's coffee while they waited. Feeling, more than watching, the sun peek over the top of tree-studded hills in a hazy sun warming morning, they sat with car doors open, feet on the gravel, backs to each other, conversing idly, comfortable with each other once again.

"Would have been nice to spend the night down here," Amy commented.

"I did try to find a place, but they were full up. Thought we could putter around town or hike in the park tomorrow."

Amy grunted in assent. The rental lurked in the back of her mind. Ted and Leonard were working alone today. Now that she had mentally written the business off to be sold, she didn't worry quite so much about it. The income sheet had to look good to potential buyers, but it had ceased to be her number one priority.

Deb's quiet voice broke into her thoughts. "Amy, look."

Amy saw Marge assembling her bike across the parking lot. "Oh boy," she breathed. Taking in Marilyn, who was also putting her bike together, she remarked, "I met that woman when I joined the bike club. Her name's Marilyn something or other." Realizing the link, she said, "Marilyn — that's the name of the woman John's with. Comes the light. Kind of slow, aren't I? Now what?"

"Now we all ride together, that's what." And hope we get along all right, Deb added to herself.

Smiling at the sight of Marge, Amy realized again how much she missed her children. "Looks good, doesn't she?"

Deb agreed, "She would have a hard time not looking good."

"Think I should go over?"

"You better. I'll stay here and watch."

Heart pounding in anticipation of rejection, Amy walked toward her daughter, who was bent over her bike unaware of her mother's presence. Marilyn looked at Amy, started to say something, then stopped.

"Hi, Marge," Amy spoke softly.

Marge's head came up and, face flushed, gray eyes startled, she stared at her mother. "You belong to the bike club, Mom?" she asked without thinking.

Amy nodded. "How are you, honey? It's so good to see you. I miss you. I never know how much until I see you again." Amy clenched her hands into fists in the pockets of her shorts.

Standing upright so that she had to look down at her mother, Marge said the first thing that came to mind. "And I forget how little you are." It sounded stupid to her. "I was going to call you or drop in at the rental."

"Really? That would be wonderful. I hope you'll still do it." It was difficult not to touch Marge, but she knew better than to make the first move.

"My transfer came through. I'm moving to Milwaukee. I'm going to live with Chris."

Chris had told Amy over the phone about this possibility earlier in the week, so it wasn't a complete surprise. "How nice for both of you."

"Where are you parked?" Marge asked, looking behind her.

Amy knew the instant Marge saw Deb. Tensing inside, she gritted her teeth.

"Do you know Marilyn?" Marge asked, wrenching her attention away from Deb and recalling the other woman's presence.

"I met you at the August meeting, didn't I?" Amy asked, reaching for Marilyn's hand.

"Yes, I should have known who you were then. You two look so much alike," she said, indicating Marge with a glance.

"She resembles her dad, too, don't you think?" Taking an immediate liking to Marilyn, Amy thought John had good taste in women.

"I guess she does," Marilyn agreed. "We're in for a long, tough ride today. These hills will probably do me in."

"They follow with vans to pick up the stragglers, don't they?" Amy asked.

Thinking this whole scene was unreal, Marge leaned against Marilyn's car and watched the two women. Again she shot a look at Deb, who was talking to some people parked near her. The anger toward Deb had abated, just as the fury directed at her mother had diminished, replaced by a bad taste and a need for distance. Listening to Amy's voice, she longed to shut her eyes and turn back the years.

"Well, what did you think of the other woman?" Deb asked, throwing a leg over her bike. They were all getting on their bikes, shoulder to shoulder in the parking lot like a herd of cattle ready to move.

"There are too many people here for me," Amy said uneasily. She hated crowds. "I like her. I did when I first met her," she answered. "John lucked out when he got her."

"Does it bother you — her and John?"

"No, I'm glad. I don't have to feel guilty anymore."

The bikes started moving out on State Road 46. Traffic slowed to a crawl and passed warily. Amy, enveloped by a mass of moving humanity, thought if one person fell, they'd all topple over like dominoes. "I don't like this," she called to Deb.

"We'll string out soon. Fall back, let those behind pass." Deb concentrated on keeping her bike out of the paths of other bikes.

"How?" A desperateness seized Amy.

Shortly, though, those behind started to flow around the two of them and they retreated to the back row. That wasn't easy for Amy, either, because she normally pedaled at full speed.

"Take it easy," Deb cautioned. "There's a long way to go and a lot of hills to climb."

"I am," Amy commented dryly, but she felt better as the gap between them and the bunched riders ahead lengthened. Marge and Marilyn were among those ahead, and, knowing Marge's penchant for speed, she wondered if she was with the front riders. Soon, when Marge moved, there'd be three hundred miles between the two of them. "I don't want Marge to move away, and I really hate to let her go while we're still so far apart."

"Maybe you can help her move, drive with her or something," Deb suggested, already puffing. Where was her endurance?

"What's the matter, Deb?" Amy asked, casting a

grin at her and quickly returning her gaze to the road. They wheeled onto a narrow blacktop road beyond the park.

"Nothing," Deb replied tersely. "You get more exercise than I do is all. You know you do."

"A little touchy about this, aren't you?" Amy grinned widely, suddenly feeling terrific. Biking always gave her a sense of control over her body.

True enough, Deb thought ruefully. Here she was more than ten years younger, supposedly something of a jock, yet obviously not as fit as Amy, and already showing signs of fatigue.

Marge rode effortlessly. At Marilyn's request she had left her far behind, and, as her mother had speculated, she was in the first few rows and still passing.

Another young woman gained on her and drew abreast. "I watched your back as long as I could."

There were only men ahead of them.

Startled, Marge glanced at the other girl, whom she judged to be about her age although shorter and heavier. Gay, was her first thought. Since Amy had left home to live with another woman, Marge had become obsessed about who was gay and who was straight. She increased her efforts to pull away, but the woman stayed with her. A smile tugged at Marge's mouth. "You ride a lot, don't you?"

"Every day. And you?"

"Sometimes I run instead," Marge admitted.

"My name's Kathy Louman. Are you a new member?"

"Marge Netzger." Marge threw her another look — observing curly brown hair, brown eyes, red cheeks sprinkled with freckles, a generous mouth. "I'm here with a member — Marilyn Holder. Do you know her?"

Kathy shook her head. "It's a big club. She a good friend?"

"My dad's fiancée," Marge replied.

"Where do you live?"

"The north side of Indianapolis, but I'm being transferred to Milwaukee soon." Thinking the other girl would now look for someone else, she noted with surprise the pleased look on Kathy's face.

"No kidding? What a coincidence. I'm moving to Milwaukee at the end of the month. I graduated from IUPUI last spring and I've got a job waiting for me in Milwaukee. And I thought I wouldn't know anyone."

Oh Christ, wouldn't you know it, Marge thought, taking another look at Kathy. "I'm going to live with my sister."

"I'm going to be on my own. Scares me silly," she added, not appearing the least bit frightened. "My mother's already shedding tears. I think it'll be harder on her than me."

"What are you going to do?"

"I'm a nurse. What do you do?"

"You had to go so far away to find a job? I canvas schools for a textbook company."

"I like Wisconsin. My family's originally from there. Lots of lakes."

Marge looked around her at the hills, feeling less threatened. Kathy appeared to be only friendly and harmless. "Are you alone today?"

"Yeah. I know a lot of the members, though. Do you cross-country ski at all?"

"Oh sure, but there's not enough snow to do much of it here."

"Well, you'll love Wisconsin then. It's great for that."

Marilyn dropped back through the bikers until she met Amy and Deb, who, now that the others were far enough ahead, were putting on speed. At least, Amy was attempting to increase the pace. Deb had discovered a reserve within herself but still found it difficult to keep up with Amy. She was greatly relieved to realize Marilyn fit her biking capabilities.

Marilyn asked, "Can I join you two? I can't keep up with Marge. I don't do this every day. I do it more for fun than anything else."

Amy grinned. "The pleasure is ours." She introduced the two women, wondering how much Marilyn knew about her relationship with Deb. Had John enlightened her? Had Marge?

"Hi. I'd shake your hand but I'd probably fall off."

"So would I," Deb said with a warm smile.

"Marge is a lovely person. So are Chris and David," Marilyn panted.

"Thanks. It's nice you get along well with them," Amy replied, assuming Marilyn did. Why wouldn't she?

"I feel more like their contemporary than anything else."

Wondering if that had been a slip of the tongue, Deb said, "I suppose you do."

"I don't know if I'm going to be able to finish this ride," Marilyn gasped, as they climbed another hill.

Deb hunched over her handlebars and grunted, "I don't either. It's a little humiliating."

Knowing she would finish, Amy shifted down. Both Deb and Marilyn stood to put more leverage on the pedals.

Around noon Marge and Kathy re-entered Brown County State Park and stopped in a meadow near a fire tower, the designated meeting spot for lunch. Marge flopped in the sun-warm grass.

"Do you mind company?" Kathy asked hesitantly, still holding her bike up.

"Not at all." And she didn't. They had laughed a lot that morning. Marge couldn't remember having as much fun with anyone other than Chris. She wondered what Chris would make of Kathy.

Kathy set her bike down next to Marge's. "There's a pop machine near the tower. What do you want? It's on me."

"Thanks." Marge clasped her legs with both arms and squinted up at Kathy. She felt content with the day.

They fell asleep in the warm sun. Marge awoke when Marilyn grabbed one of her toes. Blurry-eyed, she sat up and shook herself, and Kathy opened her eyes.

Marge said to Marilyn, "I thought maybe you got lost. You look beat." Beyond Marilyn were her mother and Deb. Deb also appeared bushed but Amy didn't. Marge smiled. "You're still riding a lot, Mom, huh?"

Pushing her bike closer, her legs vibrating pleasantly, Amy smiled.

Marilyn slumped to the grass in exhaustion with Deb nearby. "I'm starved. I could collapse and never get up. Where are the sandwiches?" she asked Marge.

"Are you going to finish, Deb?" Marilyn asked after eating. She lay back among the dandelions and covered her eyes with an arm, then glanced out from under it at Deb who was stretched between Marilyn and Amy.

"I'm going to try," was Deb's reply. It was a matter of pride.

The September day enfolded them in its warmth. The sun, covered only occasionally by fluffy white clouds, still gave off considerable heat. It was one of those wonderful fall days — the light mellow, the breeze soft, the rustling foliage beginning to show red and yellow and orange among the green. If it could only be bottled and taken out in February as a reprieve from winter, Amy thought.

They sped down a steep hill only to struggle up another — gears shifting, chains jangling, tires humming, breathing labored. Deb and Marilyn had dropped behind. Amy still had Marge and Kathy in sight but soon she would be alone among the curves and hills, which would be fine with her. She'd love to stop and listen to the sounds of birds and squirrels and humming insects, but she had this urge to maintain her position among the riders.

Back at the park entrance, Marge and Kathy leaned against Kathy's Camry waiting for the others to make their appearance.

"So when are you moving?" Kathy asked, running a brush over her sweat-dampened curls.

"I don't know when everything will be finalized."

"Hey, would you like to go to a movie tonight? Maybe get a pizza first?"

The hesitation in her voice made Marge reluctant to decline outright. "I don't know. Aren't you tired?"

"Well, yeah, but I have to eat and there are some good movies out."

"Maybe some other time."

Kathy nodded and smiled slightly.

When Deb and Marilyn straggled into the parking lot to join Amy and the two girls, Amy suggested, "Maybe we should all get something to eat before we go home."

"The Brown County Inn down the road?" Marilyn asked.

They got a table under the heavy chandeliers and antiques that crowded the rafters. Amused and heartened by Marge's reaction to Kathy, Deb listened to the talk. Marilyn, bubbling and friendly, kept the conversation going whenever it lagged. Unusually quiet, Amy let the tired, pleasant aftermath of the ride settle over her. It was a treat to hear and watch her daughter, who had been estranged from her so long.

And Marge, entertained by Kathy's wit and humor, laughed and talked and enjoyed herself as she hadn't since her mother left home. She, too, took in Amy with a hunger which left her in no doubt as to how much she had missed her mother.

When they departed in their respective cars, Kathy and Marge exchanged numbers.

XI

"Hi, it's me — Kelly. I'm having a little party, sort of a spur of the moment thing. Thought you and Deb might like to attend."

Looking out her office window — she had been about to go help Ted with customers when the phone rang — she spied Alan Young lounging against the counter. The last person she wanted to see. "It's good to hear from you, Kelly."

"The party's Saturday night, around six-thirty or whenever you can get there. I'd like to meet Deb. Brian will be there with his latest."

"I haven't talked to him for a while."

"You haven't forgotten us, have you?"

Did she just use these friends when she and Deb weren't getting along? Shamed by the thought, she protested, "I've just been busy. Can we bring anything Saturday night?"

"Just yourselves."

Amy went to the counter because Ted needed help.

"Busy today," Young commented.

"Yeah, we're busy. What do you need?" She struggled to keep the dislike out of her voice.

"I'll wait till you're done with them others here."

Wondering what he had in mind now, she glared at him. Did he want another reward? Why hadn't he just sold the stuff? It would have been a hell of a lot more lucrative. "Who's next?"

"I am, Amy."

"Paula, what brings you here?" She hadn't seen Paula since she began avoiding Jane. "I mean, I didn't expect to see you. What's up?" Stop babbling, Amy told herself.

"We're moving to the east side, closer to work. We need a truck."

How nice it would be not to have to worry about running into Jane anymore, Amy thought.

"Just had a twelve foot Ryder come in this morning," Ted said. "Mike at Ryder said we could let it go locally over the weekend."

"The truck is yours," Amy said to Paula. "Maybe we can get together one of these days." Knowing it was just one of those things she said without really intending to follow through.

"Come on into my office, Alan." Thankfully, the

colder weather forced him to wear a shirt. She squelched a shudder and closed the door. "I suppose you've found more of my equipment?" she asked.

He looked at his shoes and shuffled a little under her gaze. "Well, you ain't paying much for what I find," he complained. He reached into his shirt pocket and took out a cigarette.

"Not here. Don't smoke in my office." Sudden anger shook her. "Alan, I've had enough of this shit. I know you took the equipment you're selling back to me. If you try a stunt like that again, I'll nail you to the wall if it's the last thing I do." Stick the rest of the fucking stuff up your ass, she wanted to say, but a lifetime of inhibiting politeness prevented her from voicing the words.

He sputtered a denial. "Just trying to help you out."

"I'll help you into jail if you bother me anymore."

"Guess I'll have to rent from Rolly's," he snarled.

"Good. Why don't you do that. Now I've got things to do." Let the insurance company deal with him, she thought, dismissing him from her mind as soon as he left the office.

At the dinner table that night, Amy remarked to Deb, "You didn't tell me Jane and Paula were moving this weekend." She was more interested than she cared to admit. Was there still something going on?

Looking uncomfortable, Deb replied, "I know how you feel about me seeing Jane, and I'm helping them move. How did you find out anyway?"

"Paula reserved a truck today. She said they were moving to be closer to their jobs."

"I'd think you'd be glad to see the last of them."

"I won't miss Jane."

Deb sighed. "Can't we bury it, Amy?"

"Can we?"

"There's nothing there anymore. The more I'm with Jane the more I wonder why it happened. Want to buy a sailboat for next summer? Now would be the time to do it."

"I'm not buying anything until I'm sure we're going to be together to use it." After all, she and Deb hadn't been together very long when Deb had become involved with Jane. What would prevent it from happening again? She hardened herself to the hurt in Deb's eyes.

"How can you ever be sure? You left John after twenty-some years," Deb challenged her.

"Well, I didn't cheat on him until those twenty-some years."

"You once said you understood."

"I did not."

"Yes, you did."

Had she? "Anyway, what I really wanted to tell you is we're invited to a dinner party at Kelly's Saturday night. She wants to meet you. Will you be able to make it, since you'll be moving Jane and Paula?" Amy asked, irritated by the attempted deception.

"I'll just tell them when I have to leave. Tell me about Kelly." She wouldn't admit to being nervous about meeting Kelly, but she was.

"You'll like her. She's an interesting woman."

"You could have had her, I bet." The green in Deb's eyes suffused with a cloudiness.

"I didn't want her."

"That's consoling to hear," Deb remarked

sarcastically. "You don't want me to see Jane, yet you admit Kelly is after you and you still see her."

Taking her dishes to the kitchen, Amy retorted, "Don't jump at just any excuse, Deb. I haven't seen her since you climbed into the shower with me." Who had started the sniping? She had an uncomfortable feeling it was herself.

"I think we need another shower right about now," Deb remarked.

Amy laughed. Deb usually kept her distance after an argument. It was Amy who found lovemaking an ideal way to make up.

Brian and Douglas, Amy and Deb, Sheila and Bonnie, Kelly and Barbara sat at Kelly's table. Curious, maybe even a little jealous, Amy wanted to know Barbara's connection to Kelly. A friend filling out the couples, or were she and Kelly involved? If they were, it had to be recent or maybe it was old and revived. The woman certainly was amply endowed. Amy found it difficult to keep her eyes off Barbara's breasts. Barbara's faded brown hair was long and tied back, her eyes a light, piercing, rather disconcerting blue, her skin tanned.

Brian had introduced Douglas to Amy and Deb earlier as his doctor and told them about their first meeting. "I'm sitting in his office getting angrier by the waiting minute. There's nothing I hate more than waiting, you know. My time's worth as much as anyone's. So when he walks in half-an-hour late, I snap at him. What did I say, Douglas?"

"Something like: 'Who the fuck do you think you

are to keep me waiting so long?' " Douglas drawled, a half-smile on his face. His hair had more gray in it than black, and his ascetic face was lined with wrinkles. He was lean and tall and distinguished-looking.

Amy and Deb's faces registered amused shock. How many times had they been kept cooling their heels and not mustered the nerve to respond with the anger they had felt?

"And what was your reply to what Brian said about waiting?" Deb turned expectantly toward Douglas.

"I said I was sorry but someone was dying in the other room and since he looked so fucking healthy I thought he could wait. Parden the word, ladies."

"And I asked since this was the first time he had laid eyes on me how could he know I was so fucking healthy," Brian added.

"Well, I see somehow you found some likeable qualities in each other," Amy observed.

"When we stopped bristling and I noticed how goddamn good-looking he was," Brian said with a disarming grin. Then: "You girls look good. Make up time, huh?"

Deb and Amy exchanged sheepish grins.

"Way to go. I'm glad to see it."

"Tell me about Barbara," Amy demanded.

"I don't know any more about her than you probably do," Brian had admitted, lowering his voice a notch. "Kelly introduced her as an old friend."

During dinner Barbara was easily the quietest participant. Amy, sitting next to Brian on one side and Bonnie on the other, eyed Barbara, who was across from her. Sheila, expounding on a recent civil rights case she had lost, droned on like an annoying insect in her ears.

When there was a pause, Brian jumped into it. "What do you do, Barbara?" he asked.

All eyes gravitated to Barbara, who sat between Douglas and Deb. Appearing startled, she answered in a soft, deep voice. "I'm a writer."

"You don't know who this is then?" Kelly broke in, smiling indulgently at Barbara.

Again Amy felt a twinge of jealousy.

"Tell us," Brian insisted.

"You want to tell them or do you want me to?" Kelly asked.

"You go ahead," Barbara, modestly looking at her plate, replied in that quiet husky voice.

Unreasonably annoyed, Amy decided she didn't like this woman.

"Barbara's here to autograph books tomorrow. Didn't any of you get my mailings?"

"We did, Sheila and I did," Bonnie remarked. "I thought you all knew." In the soft overhead light Bonnie appeared less brassy, her hair almost halo-like around her made-up face. Sheila aggressively affirmed that Bonnie belonged to her with a hand on Bonnie's hand, an arm around her shoulders, a protective glance in her direction, or a few possessive words.

"Where do you live, Barbara, and how long are you staying?" Amy asked.

"I live in New York but I grew up in southern Indiana." That accounted for the drawl. "I'm staying until Tuesday."

"What's your book about?" Deb inquired. This was the first time she had met a writer.

"Three women and their relationships to each other and the more peripheral characters. You'll have to read it for more details." Barbara laughed as softly as she spoke.

"It must be exciting to put up your visiting authors, Kelly," Amy said, curious to know whether Barbara was staying with Kelly.

"Oh, it is. I get to talk about my favorite subject — books." She met Amy's eyes with a friendly smile. "I'm trying to get Barbara to move back to Indiana."

What the hell was the matter with her? Amy wondered. She should wish the best for Kelly.

Kelly went on, her eyes on Amy, "I knew Barbara at college. I was impressed with her then. I think there's a part of everyone that wants to be a writer. There is in me."

On the drive home, Deb challenged Amy. "What was going on back there? Were you jealous of Barbara or what?"

"I didn't like her. She struck me as a phony."

"Oh, come on, Amy. I thought she was very modest."

"False modesty."

"A little judgmental, aren't you? Or didn't you like her being with Kelly?"

"I just didn't care for her is all. But I did like Douglas, didn't you?"

"Yeah, he seems to be just what Brian needs."

It snowed the second week of November, a heavy six inch accumulation. Cars and trucks skidded in the rental parking lot, and Leonard was kept busy clearing the white stuff off the blacktop when he wasn't readying equipment.

Staring out the front windows at the mounds of white snow, Amy couldn't get Marge off her mind. Marge had moved at the end of October, and Amy had helped by driving a van with Marge's bulkier possessions to Milwaukee.

Chris had made room for Marge in her apartment, and she and Marge and Amy, assisted by Kathy, had unloaded the stuff and carried it up two flights of stairs.

Later, the four of them went to a Chinese restaurant for dinner. It was there that Marge told her she and Kathy had met Brian.

"He thought I was you," Marge said. "He and Douglas bought us dinner."

"How did you like him?" Amy asked, a faint smile playing around her mouth. Brian had already told her about meeting Marge and Kathy.

"He's funny, isn't he, Kath?" Marge turned to Kathy, who nodded and smiled. "Where did you meet him, Mom?"

Silently, Amy noted the abbreviation of Kathy's name. "At work." Brian seemed such a part of her life that Amy was surprised, in retrospect, at how little time had passed since they first met.

"He thinks a lot of you," Kathy said.

"He got me through some difficult times," Amy confessed.

No one asked what difficult times. Amy knew that her daughters assumed the difficult times had to do with her break from their father and home, something they preferred not to discuss with Amy.

The entire weekend in Milwaukee Amy had missed Deb. It was, Amy realized, as if she lived two lives — one with Deb and one with her own family — and these existences could never merge.

The phone rang. "You know anyone who does parking lots?" It was Brian. "I can't even get into mine."

She said, "Why don't you cancel your appointments and go home to bed. That's where Deb is — lucky woman." How she wished she were there with her. "How are you and Douglas?"

"Great. And you and Deb?"

"The same."

"You knew Barbara moved in with Kelly, didn't you?"

"She told me." Did he know how displeased she had been with that news? She couldn't have said why. Had she lost an opportunity she should have taken or was it because she had such an unusual dislike for Barbara?

"Don't keep me waiting too long, sweetie," Brian said. "Let's get together soon."

"Okay, Brian. Talk to you later."

The remainder of the day caused her to wonder why she hadn't tried to sell in the fall. Ted and Leonard both left to work on broken machinery, and she had to brave the elements to fill trucks and tractors, to check large equipment in and out. The temperature dropped like a stone all day, until at two p.m. it hovered around ten degrees above zero. The diesels still unstarted that day refused to start.

She couldn't wait to get inside the building. Her hands and feet and face felt frozen. Wind whipped the top layer of now icy snow around like white fog. Thinking she heard the outside telephone bell ringing, she ran for the door.

"Amy, how's it going?" It was John.

"It just took me an hour to start one of the skid loaders and get it on a trailer, and I can't hear the phone out there because of the wind."

"I can't come over right now. Too many claims. A client's house burned down this morning."

Why the hell had he called then? she asked herself. "Maybe I should get Deb over here to help." Would he object?

"Do what you have to do," he said curtly. He wouldn't go to the rental that day.

An eager learner, Deb answered the phone with an assuredness she did not feel. Paging through the card catalog or the Ryder rental sheets, she dispensed information and grew more confident with each call.

Deb's presence freed Amy to wait on customers inside and outside. It was nice to re-enter the building and see Deb behind the counter. "If you worked with me, I might not sell come spring." She knew that wasn't true. It was time to sell while there was still a profit to make.

"I like this," Deb replied. "I'd consider working here."

"It's too late now. The advertising has gone out." Amy, hoping they'd seen the last customer, leaned on the counter and soaked up the warmth. It was a half hour to closing and neither Ted nor Leonard had returned.

The next call was from Ted.

"I'm at the hospital." He rushed his explanation

before she could ask for it. "Leonard collapsed when we were pulling the loader tractor onto the trailer with the crawler. He fell face first on the crawler and it just kept going. I got to it when it hit a big tree." Ted laughed nervously. It was a habit of his to cover his distress with laughter. "I pulled the emergency brake on the loader and jumped off. You should see Leonard's face. It hit the front panel."

"What hospital? And how is he?" Her thoughts raced wildly and kept returning to the question: Why did something always have to go wrong?

"St. Vincent's, but I don't know how he is. The rescue wagon brought us here. I need to go back and get the machinery."

"I'll be right there. You can drive my car back to the equipment."

She careened along Eighty-Sixth Street toward St. Vincent's. Vehicles crept along the icy street, and, occasionally going into a heart-stopping skid, she passed them. She spoke to Ted only long enough to find where Leonard had been taken.

Hurrying along the corridors of the hospital, she allowed herself to think of Leonard, who lived alone. Leonard had worked for her nearly from the beginning, and she felt an unspoken fondness for him. He had been part of their holiday celebrations, because he had no immediate family in the area. How old was he? she asked herself as she reached the emergency rooms and tried to extract information from a nurse behind a desk.

The nurse gave her a kindly look. "Are you a relative?"

"Not a blood relative, but he's been a part of my family for years. Please, how is he?"

The nurse led her into a room where a man in scrubs, whom Amy assumed was a doctor, met her.

Glancing in the open door behind the doctor, she saw what looked like a replica of Leonard lying on a white table, wires strung from his chest to an electrocardiograph on the wall. Her eyes watched the lines move horizontally across the screen. "Leonard?" She turned to the doctor, her eyes questioning him.

"Are you related to this man?"

She shook her head. "He's like a part of the family, though. I don't think he has any relatives here."

"He suffered a massive coronary. We tried to revive him." He moved aside as she walked past him toward Leonard.

Staring down at Leonard's bruised face, she noticed the colorless eye. There was no mistaking death. Was it the soul that gave light and color to the eyes? Whatever it was, it had fled the body. Touching the older man's arm set off the tears. "Oh, Leonard," she whispered.

Blindly she walked out to the hall and into John, who was giving information to the doctor. Behind her grief, she wondered how they would get through the winter at the rental without Leonard. John took her by both arms and then hugged her to him, causing her to cry harder. He could still be a comfort. She knew he would take care of all the necessary details. Her arms slipped around John as she sobbed for the loss of the man on the table, for not being a better friend to him. Like so many faithful friends, she had tended to take him for granted.

* * * * *

To assuage their depression over Leonard's death, Marge and Chris planned with Kathy a spur of the moment cross-country ski weekend in the Upper Peninsula, where more than a foot of snow had fallen.

The trails were ungroomed and surface frozen, not good conditions in any weather. Saturday the wind combined with frigid temperatures discouraged all but the most stalwart. The three young women, whose skis broke through the icy top layer with every glide, sweated under their clothes while their faces burned with cold. They struggled along, finished a looping trail, and dove into the waiting car.

"Jesus Christ, I'm not that desperate to ski," Marge said between chattering teeth.

"I'm not either," Kathy agreed.

"Okay, you wimps, let's go find some other form of entertainment," Chris said, glad she didn't have to admit her sudden lack of enthusiasm for the outdoors.

That night Chris met a young man. He ventured to their table and introduced himself and sat with them. Later Kathy and Marge returned to the motel without Chris, whom they left dancing with the young man.

At the motel Kathy turned on the television and, stretched out on their respective beds, she and Marge watched *The Breakfast Club* on cable.

"I loved this movie," Marge remarked.

"I did too." Kathy lay with arms behind her head.

Feeling herself observed, Marge glanced over at

the other bed and met Kathy's dark troubled gaze. "What's wrong?"

"I like you," Kathy said quietly.

"That's nice. I like you too," Marge replied. Then said, "Oh . . . you mean . . ." She flushed with understanding.

Kathy nodded mutely.

"I'm not that way, Kathy. Sorry."

Looking embarrassed, Kathy swung her feet over the edge of the bed and sat up. "I'm the one who's sorry."

"It's okay," Marge said, wishing Kathy hadn't brought this up. "My mother is." Was it hereditary?

"Forget I said anything," Kathy begged. "Really. Can you forget what I said and not tell Chris?"

"Of course. It's forgotten. We can still be friends, can't we?" Marge smiled, feeling more smug than threatened. Glancing surreptitiously at Kathy, who did not return the look, Marge wondered briefly what it would be like. She would never do such a thing, she told herself. She wasn't like her mother and never would be.

A key turned in the lock. An icy blast of air shot into the room with Chris.

"Goddamn, it's cold. That fool wanted to neck in the car in this cold. Why do they always assume you want to do it?" She stomped her frozen feet on the carpet and shrugged out of her ski jacket. Her dark eyes flashed with anger; her cheeks were bright and cold.

Irritated, Marge spoke sharply. "You pick up some guy and you expect him not to come on to you? Get real, Chris. This is the eighties."

"What have you two been up to?" Chris asked,

not put off by her sister's annoyance. Her interest was aroused when she saw Kathy blush and glance nervously at Marge. She had meant nothing by the question. Later she would ask Marge again and not be entirely satisfied with Marge's answer.

An early winter wrapped an icy fist around the Great Lakes states, including Indiana. Increasingly, Amy hated going out into the dark frigid mornings, where the cold breathed ice into her lungs and froze her nostrils together. Now that Leonard was gone, she often found herself forced outside to help a customer when Ted was delivering or repairing equipment. A lengthy depression had settled over her like a heavy blanket, and so far she had been unable to shrug it off or even pin it down. Her sense of humor had always seemed to have a life of its own; she'd never completely lost it when she had broken with her family, nor when Deb had been involved with Jane. But recently, casting about for a ray of hope, she could only find bleakness ahead of her.

By spring the rental business would be sold if the feelers coming from various parts of the country were any indication. What would she do once she was free of the constraints of the rental? As appealing as her impending freedom appeared to be, the worry about its cost loomed in her mind. She would have to find a job. She hadn't worked for anyone but herself since her marriage. What kind of job should she look for? Business management? But — hadn't she failed with her own business? She turned these thoughts around in her mind without resolution.

And then there was Deb. Their relationship was a shambles.

Tired, because she had been unable to sleep last night, Amy envisioned a day when she and Deb separated, when the reason for leaving her family disappeared from her life. If they could just reach for each other as they once had and bury their differences in lovemaking — but they couldn't even do that anymore.

Whenever they made love, Amy wondered what it had been like for Deb to make love with Jane. She had gone so far as to ask, and Deb had refused to discuss it. Resentment had stolen into her feelings for Deb. Lovemaking was now infrequent and unsatisfying. And Amy became more miserable with each passing day.

Amy leaned on the counter and listened to the wind howling around the building, seeking cracks and crevices through which to enter. Ted was out picking up a backhoe, leaving her alone to deal with whatever customers braved the elements to show up at the rental.

When work was over, as much as she wanted the day to end, she dreaded returning to the apartment. Was that any way to live? She called Brian's number but there was no answer. She hurried to her car, which she had started earlier to warm it. But she didn't drive home. Instead she turned in the direction of Broad Ripple.

Deb was already home when Amy left work. Restless, unable to sit for any length of time, she had started dinner and fixed a couple drinks and put them in the freezer. Now she stood staring out the patio door at the darkness, hearing the wind moan and rage at the building. The smell of slowly cooking chili filled the apartment. Where the hell was Amy? It was eight, long past time for her return. Did she not want to come home? Neither had she herself.

She lay across the bed and didn't hear Amy let herself into the apartment, because the television was on.

Amy stood in the doorway of the bedroom. Gingerly she sat on the bed and touched Deb's back, causing Deb to emit a small scream and spring to her feet. "Sorry. I didn't mean to scare you."

"Jesus, why are you sneaking around?" Deb's heart hammered in her chest.

"I'm not. I wasn't trying to be quiet. It smells good. Chili?"

A sheepish smile stole across Deb's face. "You really frightened me." A scowl replaced the grin. "Why are you so late?"

Amy replied honestly, "I was driving around, listening to the radio."

"Not wanting to come home, right?"

"Right. Seems like all we do is argue anymore."

A sudden thought came to Deb. Brian had once said they should separate and get their heads on straight. Perhaps he had been right.

"Maybe I should move out for a while. Stay with my mother."

Amy stiffened, held in the grip of strong emotions, one following another in rapid succession. The first one was fear of being alone, fear of the loneliness of the apartment. Next came a surprising sensation of freedom as she imagined answering to no one, doing whatever she wanted to do. Then she felt a sense of loss so keen it was physical. Had they lost each other in mutual recriminations? She met Deb's eyes which were troubled mirrors of her own. She shrugged. "If that's what you want, Deb."

The offer to leave spoken, Deb would have given anything to take the words back. But Amy hadn't argued. Deb responded glumly, "Maybe we need some time apart." Say no, she silently urged Amy.

Instead Amy said, "Maybe we do."

XII

The sun hid behind glowering clouds. Whenever John and Marilyn stepped outside with a piece of furniture, a cold wind attacked. A confused Grit ran worried circles as they struggled with beds and couch and chairs. And when everything was moved out and into their new home and he and Marilyn were left alone to clean the house in which John and Amy had lived more than twenty years, John stood in the empty kitchen and said a silent goodbye. He was not one to dwell on past mistakes or memories, but so much of his life had been spent in this house.

"Are you sorry, John?" Marilyn asked, coming into the room and putting an arm around him.

He pulled her to him and shook his head. "Not really. It's like closing a door on something and opening a new one. Sounds corny, doesn't it?"

It was her turn to shake her head. "It's exactly like that. There are a lot of memories and years in this house for you," she said softly.

"Yeah, and a lot of the memories are good ones, but I'm looking forward to you and me. Let's get this place cleaned and get out of here."

The back door opened and Amy stepped into the kitchen. Uncertain of her welcome, she gave them a strained smile. "I just had to see the place once more. I'm sorry."

Marilyn rushed into the awkwardness. "Hell, don't be sorry. You're just in time to help — that is, if you want to."

"Why not one more time," Amy said, and walked through the bare rooms. She was amazed at how little sadness the empty house generated in her.

When the cleaning was over, the three of them went to Country Kitchen and ate a late supper. Amy had not eaten since breakfast and was queasy with hunger. Since Deb had moved out, she had lost ten pounds she could ill afford to lose.

"How's Deb?" Marilyn asked after they were comfortably ensconced in a booth.

"Good." She didn't know whether Deb was all right or not. They had talked by phone just that morning and Deb had said she was fine and had asked how Amy was, and Amy had lied and professed to be fine herself — whatever fine was.

Observing his ex-wife carefully, John noticed the signs of depression he had seen on other occasions during their years together — dark splotches under the eyes which were cloudy with preoccupation, a listlessness she could not quite hide.

Later, when he and Marilyn were wrapped around each other in bed, Marilyn commented on Amy. "She's not happy right now, is she?"

"Who?" he asked, knowing who.

"Amy. I like her, John."

"Good. We're all linked together through the kids." He kissed her softly on the neck, then on the cheek, and moved on to her mouth.

"I wish I could help her," she said through the kiss, her voice muffled.

"Don't get carried away," he said, his hands caressing her bare back.

The wind pushed Deb's Subaru as she turned onto Ridge Road and drove past the apartment, which was dark. She entered the parking lot but Amy's car was gone. She parked in the spot reserved for their apartment and for a few minutes contemplated waiting for Amy's return. Much as she longed to see Amy, she feared the feelings Amy generated in her. She knew she ought to make a decision soon, whether to attempt a reconciliation or move to her own place. Living with her mother was no solution.

Leaving Ridge Road behind, she drove to the nearest McDonald's. Even the strangers eating Big Macs and french fries around her in the brightly lit room were company of sorts. Now that she no longer lived with Amy, strange how Jane was drifting out of her life. Too bad she hadn't been able to let it happen sooner. Hunched over her salad, wrapped in her thoughts, she didn't notice Kelly until the older woman sat across the table from her.

"Deb, isn't it?" Kelly asked, eyeing her with what Deb interpreted as kind interest.

Surprised, Deb said, "You're one person I never expected to see in McDonald's."

"I have a secret passion for their french fries," Kelly admitted. "How have you been?"

"Okay, and you and Barbara?" Was that a safe question to ask? Perhaps Barbara had flown the coop as she had.

"We're fine. I haven't seen Amy for a while. How is she?"

Deb sighed deeply, trying to decide whether to comment on their split or not. "I talked to her this morning and she said she was fine."

Looking puzzled, Kelly said, "Horrid out, isn't it? I can't believe I ventured out just for some fries. But sometimes I have to get out in the fresh air."

"We could go have a drink somewhere," Deb said.

"We can go to my place. That would be nice."

"I wasn't inviting myself, you know," Deb said with an imploring look. But she didn't want to go home yet, and she didn't want to be alone.

"Of course you weren't."

The warmth welcomed them as Kelly unlocked and opened the door to her apartment. Barbara was nowhere in sight. "What would you like to drink?"

"Anything with vodka in it, if you have vodka."

"Sure do. Is V-8 juice all right?" Kelly's head was in the refrigerator.

"Sounds good." Leaning against the kitchen door frame, Deb felt the welcome emanating from the other woman. Perhaps she was lonely too. She took the drink Kelly handed her, and they moved into the living room.

"Barbara is out of town again. She spends a lot of time on the East coast," Kelly explained.

"Did you know one time I was jealous of you?" Deb confessed.

Smiling, Kelly said, "You had no reason to be, you know. Amy told me she loved you. Would you like some chips?" She half rose out of her chair.

Deb waved her back down. "No, thanks. I have to lose a few pounds. Now that my mother's feeding me every day it's almost impossible to keep my weight down." Knowing she had just given it away, Deb licked her lips. "I don't know how Amy is because I don't live with her anymore."

"I didn't know," Kelly said quietly. "I didn't think that would ever happen."

Deb asked, "Did she talk at all about last summer?"

"Some," Kelly answered, sounding reluctant.

"We thought we survived that, but I guess in

reality we didn't." Deb wondered if she should talk about this to Kelly. What if Kelly still had an interest in Amy?

"You look pretty unhappy," Kelly said into the silence.

"I am. I'm sorry — I didn't mean to bring this into your living room."

Kelly ignored that. "I haven't seen Amy, so I don't know how she feels, but it wouldn't hurt to tell her how you feel, would it?"

"Probably not," Deb said, knowing she wouldn't. "I read Barbara's book," she said. "Has she got another one in the works?"

"She does, if she'll just stay put long enough to finish it."

Was there just a bit of anger in Kelly's voice? "She's a good writer."

"She is," Kelly agreed. "It's nice to have company. What else have you read lately?"

On the way back to her mother's, Deb again drove past the apartment where she had lived with Amy. Still no lights and no car. Where the hell was Amy?

With Christmas rapidly approaching Amy took the second weekend of December to shop. In a dismal mood she threaded her way through crowds and endured the holiday music blaring from speakers. What to buy? Always a problem, it was even more so this year with everyone scattered.

She found herself hemmed in by crowds, a jewelry display case in front of her. She noticed a gold dove pendant. She bought it and a gold chain to give to Deb. If she didn't see Deb, she would send it to her. The peaceful pleasure from the purchase enabled her to shop in earnest. She bought Christmas gifts for everyone.

And on the way home she purchased a small Scotch pine and some lights and ornaments. The pleasant aroma of the pine tree filled the rooms of the apartment.

She planned a little tree-trimming party. Maybe she could shake herself free from the dark cloud she was under. What good was her misery doing anyone, least of all herself? So she sent out invitations for dinner and a party next Saturday evening to Brian and Douglas, Kelly and Barbara, Sheila and Bonnie, and lastly Deb. She thought of inviting John and Marilyn but decided that might prove awkward all the way around. If the talk turned gay, what would John make of it? She had no doubt Marilyn would handle it with humor and aplomb.

Sending Deb an invitation cheered her as much as buying the gold dove had. It gave her hope. They would meet again under friendly circumstances, if Deb showed up, and if nothing else, she would see Deb again. There was that relatively once more. Now it would be enough just to see Deb, whereas it hadn't been enough when they had lived together. They had always expected something more or different from each other then.

Replies came in different forms. Brian called to say he and Douglas had been invited to another party that day but, of course, he'd get out of it and come to hers. "I have something for you, sweetie. I just got it today."

Consumed with curiosity she said, "Really? I can't wait."

"Want me to tell you what it is?"

"No, Brian, I like surprises."

"Good. You'll be so surprised."

Bonnie dashed off an affirmative reply on a note pad page with a heading that read: *Teachers do it best with students,* causing Amy to wrinkle her nose.

Kelly called Amy at work, saying she'd be there without Barbara — to Amy's relief — because Barbara was still out of town.

Deb wrote from school. Yes, she'd be there. It was nice to hear from Amy, and she was looking forward to seeing her. Reading and re-reading the note, Amy searched for hidden meanings and found none.

Saturday a slushy snow fell all day and by closing time Amy was frantic to leave and finish her party preparations. She'd ordered the food catered, but she had to pick it up and go home and shower and do the little things she hadn't yet done — set out dishes, tableware and napkins, arrange the hors d'oeuvres. She wanted time to relax before company arrived.

But her hair was still wet when the first knock on the door sounded, and she opened it to Brian and Kelly. Douglas had been called to the hospital on an emergency case.

Brian followed Kelly in, grinned wickedly at Amy, and thrust a squirming soft bundle into her arms. "Merry Christmas."

This must be the surprise. She didn't even like cats, and he'd brought her a kitten.

"Someone left a whole litter on my porch," he

explained, taking off his jacket and hanging it and Kelly's in the coat closet. "Thought you might like company." When Amy continued to stare silently at the small black kitten, he said, "It's not like I brought you a dog. You don't have to walk cats or housebreak them." He opened the front door and retrieved a box and a bag of kitty litter. "See? I'll even fix a potty for kitty. Where do you want it?"

Setting the kitten on the floor, Amy looked at Kelly and then Brian. "I just didn't expect this. Why me? What did I ever do to you?"

"He gave me one, too, if that helps any," Kelly said. "And he's got more to pass out to the soft-hearted."

They watched the kitten fall on its face, regain its balance and wobble around the room mewing pitifully.

"Looks kind of little to be separated from its mama," Amy remarked.

"She is. Feed her this." Brian pulled from his jacket pocket a miniature bottle and some half-and-half.

"She?" Amy repeated, picturing a yowling grown-up cat in heat.

"I'll take care of her reproductive organs when she's a little bigger. Nothing to it," Brian assured Amy.

"She is kind of cute," Kelly said. "I was about as enthusiastic as you when I received my present. What do you do to your enemies, Brian?" she asked dryly.

Another knock. Amy flung open the door to Sheila and Bonnie and Deb just behind them.

While they exclaimed over the tiny black

creature, Amy stole looks at Deb and caught Deb's eyes on her as often as she looked.

To cover her confusion, Deb scooped the baby cat off the floor and cuddled her. Brian handed her the bottle and Deb fed its contents to the kitten. "What's her name?"

"Has she got one?" Amy glanced at Brian.

"It's up to you to give her one," he said to Amy. "Nice ice-breaker, isn't she?"

"As if we need one," Sheila drawled. "We're all friends here."

"How about Briny. It's close to Brian," Bonnie suggested.

"I've got a kitten for you and Sheila, too, Bonnie."

"Are you breeding cats now, Brian?" Sheila inquired.

Amy went to the kitchen and called for drink orders. Brian followed her. "Did you see how she looks at you?" he whispered in Amy's ear.

"Who?" Amy asked.

"You'll get together again." He helped her mix drinks.

"Always an optimist, Brian. That's nice," she said, a flicker of hope rising at his words.

Deb appeared in the doorway, kitten asleep in her arms, and set the empty bottle on the counter. "Where do sleeping cats go?" she asked.

"On the floor somewhere," Amy said.

"I'm saving the last kitten for you, Deb. You can pick her up tonight."

"I live with my mother. I'd have to ask her."

"Nonsense. You're too old to ask your mother anything but what she wants for dinner."

Deb's laughter filled the kitchen. In the next room the others' voices blended to make background noise. "Anything I can do? Take this stuff out to the table?" Deb gestured at the trays of food. "Sure looks good."

When the tree hung heavy with strings of lights and brightly colored ornaments, they sat around the living room and smoked the dope Bonnie had brought for the party. "Just a little cheer," Bonnie said as soon as the room lights were out and the tree lights lit.

"And you're a principal?" Kelly asked with a husky laugh.

"If you can't beat 'em, join 'em," Bonnie said, rolling and lighting up another joint.

"Let's stay here tonight," Brian said. "You women are safe with me. Can you believe that?" He made his way to the phone and called his house, but Douglas was still gone.

Sheila said, "You're the only man here — a handsome one at that — and none of us want you either. Can you believe that?"

The next morning Amy woke up on the davenport. Deb sat in the nearby chair with the kitten in her arms. The tree lights were still lit, glasses with watered down drinks littered the room, along with plates of half-eaten food.

Holding her head with both hands, Amy sat up and looked around her. "Holy shit, what happened last night?"

It came back to her, the last couple hours fuzzily. She got to her feet and lurched down the hall. "You didn't go to Brian's to get your gift cat?" she asked Deb from the bathroom.

"I vaguely remember them leaving," Deb called back.

"Why did you stay?" Amy inquired, looking critically at her reflection while brushing her hair. Her eyes shone back red from the mirror; her hair stuck out wildly in different directions and refused to be tamed.

"We didn't want to leave you alone."

"We?" Amy called back.

"Why don't you come here and talk to me," Deb said with a trace of annoyance.

Going to her closet, Amy retrieved the wrapped packages — her Christmas purchases — including the one with the dove and chain. She carried them to the living room and set them under the tree. "Did everyone have a good time?" she asked, pulling open the drapes. Blinding sunshine flooded the room.

"A marvelous time was had by all, I guess. What do you think of this little animal?"

Amy turned and looked at Deb whose green eyes also showed red. An almost irresistible urge to run her fingers through Deb's dark cap of hair seized her — to walk over and just gently pull Deb's head against her body. What would happen? She wouldn't give in to the desire, so she'd never know. Instead, she laughed.

Deb's eyes narrowed. "What's so funny?"

"Nothing. Aren't you hungry? I'm starved."

"Maybe I should go home," Deb said, not wanting to leave. She set the kitten on a pillow on the floor and followed Amy into the kitchen where she wanted to corner her, an arm on either side, against the counter.

"Eat first. I hate eating alone. Brian woke me

from a hungover sleep to tell me he hated eating alone one morning."

"I remember that morning. I was alone, wondering where you had spent the night."

"Scrambled eggs?" Amy asked, starting the coffee.

"Sure." Deb cut up green peppers and onions to add to the eggs.

XIII

Christmas, as inevitable as death and nearly as dreaded, arrived in a cold rain. The kids came home and the girls slept at John and Marilyn's while David stayed with his mother. Christmas morning Amy and David packed up gifts and drove to John's new house. It was all so civil, Amy thought.

But first Amy called Deb to wish her Merry Christmas. At least she wouldn't have to worry about offending Deb when she spent the day with her kids and John and Marilyn. With a little encouragement Marilyn probably would have invited Deb to join them. "I have something for you, Deb," Amy said casually. "I should have given it to you the night of the party."

"I'll stop by." Deb, too, had experienced anxious moments about this day, but it was going better than she had thought it would.

Briny was less trouble than Amy had anticipated, if a little destructive in her playful enthusiasm. When not chewing on the plants, jumping at ornaments, or sharpening her claws on the furniture, she spent most of her time asleep. It was nice to have something responsive to come home to every night, even a mewling cat.

"Should we take her with us?" David asked, looking down at the kitten who was attacking his shoelaces. He carried in a flat box the pumpkin pies his mother had made for Christmas dinner.

"No, she'll be all right. Grit wouldn't like her." Amy held the kitten at arm's length while they slipped out the door.

Amy thought John and Marilyn's new house cutesy. Marilyn collected Hummels and they filled shelves in the living room. Framed poems hung on the walls; *The House By The Side Of The Road* was just inside the front door. She had to admit the place was homey, especially with a bright fire in the living room fireplace and the smell of turkey and other foods.

Marilyn and the two girls were in the kitchen working on dinner preparations. Amy arranged her gifts under the tree by the bay window in the front room and wandered to the kitchen. It was a lovely room — large and light and airy with a butcher block table between the counters at which Chris and Marge were cutting vegetables.

"Anything I can do?" Amy asked after exchanging welcomes.

"You bet," Marilyn said cheerfully. "Good to see you."

Amy poured herself and Marilyn a cup of coffee, then proceeded to peel potatoes.

"How is Kathy?" Amy asked.

"Good," Chris answered. "We've been doing a lot of skiing and stuff together. She has a crush on Marge." Looking at her sister, Chris hurriedly added, "Just teasing, Marge, I'm sorry, I wasn't thinking."

"I guess you weren't." Flinging down her cutting knife, Marge stormed out of the kitchen.

"Now I've done it. Hell and damn, I always go too far. But she didn't seem to mind until now. Should I go after her?" Chris looked worriedly in the direction her sister had taken.

"Does Kathy really have a crush on Marge?" Amy asked.

"Yeah, she does." Chris threw a questioning look at her mother.

"Go after her. See what you can do. I sure can't do it," Amy said.

"Do you want me to?" Marilyn offered hesitantly.

"Better I go." Chris left the room.

Marilyn was good at small talk, and smoothed over the family difficulties with conversation. Amy felt something akin to love for her.

"We're lucky to have you, Marilyn," Amy said.

For a few seconds Marilyn appeared overcome with emotion, then remarked in a low but cheerful voice, "I'm lucky to have a ready made family, you know. My sister's clear across the country. My mother died last year and my dad died years ago. I'm the one who's fortunate to have you all."

Chris returned with a sulky looking Marge. Chris and Marilyn and Amy pretended nothing had happened between the two young women. Marilyn broke open a bottle of champagne and mixed it with orange juice, which they all drank while readying the meal.

From the living room came the sounds of David and his father talking and laughing. After a while, drawn by the smells emanating from the kitchen, the two men joined the women.

On the way to Amy's apartment that evening, as David navigated the car through a driving rain, Amy thought how well the day had gone and that Marilyn had actually set Amy free, acting as a sort of cushion protecting members of the family from each other.

Jesus, what a day for it to rain. Deb sat in the darkened living room with only the tree lights to brighten her gloom. Looking forward all day to this time alone, Deb listened to the rain beating at the windows and watched it under the street light coming down in sheets. Never had she felt so alone. But it was better than sharing the aloneness with others.

What did Amy have for her? Deb wondered, picking up the black and white kitten Brian had given her. She had no gift for Amy and that depressed her, even though she had searched the stores. Perhaps she should hit the shops tomorrow and look for a token gift, anything. The old unspoken rule — a gift for a gift.

She turned on the television and watched *It's A Wonderful Life,* a movie she had always liked.

Tomorrow she'd visit Amy. No, Amy's kids would be around. It would be easier for Amy not to have her around right now. With that thought all her goodwill vanished and she drifted off into a restless sleep.

Revelling promised to be dangerous on New Year's Eve. An early rain turned to sleet and then snow as the day progressed and the temperature steadily dropped. Skidding home, Amy decided to stay there instead of going to John and Marilyn's party where she would be a third wheel anyway.

Briny attacked her feet as soon as she entered the apartment. Closing the door on the cold, she switched on the news. Uttering dire warnings of hazardous road conditions, the newsman urged people to celebrate the coming New Year at home. Well, why not? She'd mix something to drink, fix something good to eat, watch a little television or read a book, go to bed. She had often wondered why people felt obliged to be jolly on New Year's Eve. They would soon all be another year older. Was that something to be joyous about? Not at her age it wasn't.

Just after she had fallen asleep, a pounding at the door brought her to her feet, her heart thudding with alarm. She heard voices outside her apartment — Brian's loud, Deb's soft but unmistakable. She pulled the door open.

"Jesus, woman, it's about time," Brian said, taking in the bathrobe and disheveled hair.

She grinned at him and then glanced at Deb. Their faces were red with cold and snow glistened in their hair. "Still snowing, I see."

"Put on some clothes and we'll make a snowman," Brian commanded, his words slurred.

"Not tonight. Maybe tomorrow." Amy shut the door behind them and hugged the robe to herself.

"Got anything to drink, Amy?" Brian asked.

Amy shot a look at Deb, who shook her head which Amy misunderstood. "What are the roads like?" she asked Deb.

"Pretty bad," Deb said, trailing Amy into the kitchen. She dropped her voice to a whisper. "He and Douglas had a terrible fight. I came across him in a bar where I went with friends. That's why he's so drunk. Douglas moved out."

"Oh God." Running a hand through her hair, trying to tame it, Amy asked, "Should I fix him anything?"

"Sure. He's not driving. Maybe you can get him to stay the night."

They could hear Brian talking to Briny in the other room as if the cat were a person. "And how was your New Year's Eve? Did you lose your lover in a stupid fight over the dumbest damn thing? Well, fuck him." Then they heard the harsh sounds of tears. Frozen momentarily, they looked at each other.

"Oh shit," Amy muttered.

Deb handed Brian his drink. "I thought it was going to work this time," Brian said, no longer crying. He was slumped in an armchair.

Deb and Amy sat at opposite ends of the davenport, looking at him with concern.

Brian gave a jarring laugh. "You ought to see your faces. Don't look so goddamn worried. I'll be fine."

"Maybe it will work, Brian. What happened anyway or shouldn't I ask?"

"I don't even know what we started fighting about. He's a very demanding person. We're both demanding, as a matter of fact, set in our ways. Probably wouldn't have worked anyway." He gazed at the two women. "What about you two? Here you're consoling me and you're still apart."

Amy and Deb exchanged wary looks as if they were dangerous to each other.

"Shit happens, as they say," Brian remarked. "A good drink, Amy." He held up his glass. "How about another?"

Later, Brian fell asleep on the davenport. Amy and Deb were playing cribbage at the table, the television droning as background noise to inform them when midnight struck and New Year's Day began. Outside, snow fell thickly.

"You better stay the night, too, Deb," Amy said. After all, Deb had slept in her old bedroom after the tree trimming party.

"Maybe I should," Deb agreed.

Amy spotted the one small package safely resting on a branch in the tree to protect it from Briny. Retrieving it, Amy set it on the table.

"This for me?" Deb asked.

Amy nodded. "I thought you'd like it."

Deb had spent one whole day after Christmas searching for something for Amy and had come up empty-handed. She stared at the tiny gold dove on the chain and attempted to attach meaning to this gift. Doves being the symbol of peace, was it a peace offering? A smile spread across her face. She met Amy's eyes. "Thanks. It's lovely."

She fastened the chain around her neck and felt tears coming on. She pushed them away with words. "I like it. I love it. Thanks again."

"Looks nice on you," Amy said with a wry half smile. Deb would be forced to think of her whenever she wore the necklace. Was that why she had bought it? She still wasn't sure.

Deb said, "I don't have anything for you. I looked. I just didn't see anything appropriate."

"A gift doesn't make an obligation. I don't want anything. Buying that helped me shop. It got me moving." True enough.

For the space of a few minutes they were close enough to reach for each other, but the time for it passed. After midnight, they went to their separate rooms, leaving Brian snoring loudly on the couch.

"Maybe Douglas left him because he snores," Amy commented as she turned out the lights.

"It would make me leave," Deb said.

After Deb and Brian's departure early the next afternoon, Amy felt strangely dissatisfied. They had boxed up the ornaments and Brian had dragged the tree outside to the trash. As she vacuumed pine needles, dusted furniture and rearranged the room, it dawned on her why she had bought the gold dove and chain and why she felt so disgruntled. She had thought, although not consciously, that giving Deb the chain would somehow bring them together again. The gift had been a peace offering, and Deb had shrugged it off. Certain now they would never again be lovers, she felt despair threaten to overwhelm her.

Kelly couldn't have chosen a better time to show up at her door, Amy thought gratefully as she let her in the apartment. Forcing a smile, albeit a rather sad one, she said, "You just missed Brian and Deb."

"Too bad. It would have been fun," Kelly said, not looking at all disappointed. Her hair curled around her ruddy face. She removed steamy glasses which softened her dark eyes even more and made her appear vulnerable.

"Come on in and cheer me up. I hate New Year's."

"Oh, why?" Kelly asked, shrugging out of her jacket.

"I don't know why." Amy hung the coat in the closet. "I just always have. What did you do last night?"

"Read. It was too miserable to go out, and Barbara's out of town again. What did you do?"

Amy related last night's tale, got Kelly a can of pop, and sat on the davenport near Kelly's chair. Surprised when Kelly got up and moved next to her and even more surprised when Kelly took her hand, Amy responded with restrained interest. It appeared that Deb wanted out of her life, was in fact out of it. So why not Kelly? She liked her, thought her reasonably attractive and certainly interesting. She had to build some kind of life. Besides, she was horny as hell and had been for a long time. It was rewarding to be wanted again. For that she was just plain thankful.

But an element of excitement was missing. A part of Amy stood back and watched their love-making begin.

Kelly leaned forward and kissed her, a gentle, tentative kiss that stirred Amy to respond. She touched Amy's face softly, cupping her chin. Then her hand moved down over Amy's neck, to her breasts, barely touching. Amy trembled at the gentle exploration. She felt Kelly opening her shirt, felt her kissing the places she touched, the tugging of Kelly's mouth on her breast. When Kelly reached between her legs, Amy quivered with anticipation. No longer was a part of her watching the action. For the length of time it took her to come she belonged to Kelly.

She turned to the other woman. While she and Deb made love, sometimes Amy thought of the ways she would return the lovemaking, until desire blotted out the thinking process. She had decided now to use what she considered the old standby — the flat on the back pose, fingers caressing intimately, mouth moving across the upper part of the body.

She had always enjoyed watching Deb succumb to her touch, especially that moment when she knew there was no turning back, when she had Deb's total attention and passion. Somehow Amy couldn't quite keep Deb out of this act, no matter how she tried to push her out of her mind. The feeling that this was the wrong woman she was making love to became even stronger when Kelly moaned loudly and spoke Amy's name.

Later, when they lay in each other's arms, Kelly hugged Amy to her. "You're a good lover, Amy," she said in a husky voice.

"So are you," Amy replied quietly, wanting to move away, thinking this was a mistake. But her body felt at peace for the first time in weeks. "Want something to eat?" She started to sit up but Kelly pulled her back down, got up on an elbow, and looked Amy over critically.

"You have a nice body," she commented, running her hand over Amy's breasts, down to her navel, and further down to the dampness between her legs.

Going a little rigid, Amy refused to spread her legs, and Kelly pulled them apart with a foot.

"Let's take a shower," Amy suggested, then felt the gentle persuading touch and responded in spite of herself.

Touching the gold dove and glancing at it in the rearview mirror, Deb decided she had missed a cue when Amy had given her the necklace. Determined to finally set things right between them, she drove to Ridge Road. Rehearsing what she would say and do when face to face with Amy, she pulled into the parking lot as Kelly disappeared into the apartment building.

What the hell was going on? Kelly had said she never dropped in on anyone without calling first.

Amy must have known she was coming when Deb and Brian were there, and had said nothing.

She knew where she stood now, she thought bitterly, driving away. So something was going on between Amy and Kelly. Perhaps they were in bed together now. The thought of Amy making love to Kelly and vice versa made her feel ill and a little desperate.

A bleary-eyed Brian answered her insistent knocking. "You just left, woman. Hurry and get inside. It's colder than a witch's tit out there." He shut the door behind her and led her to the kitchen.

Unable to sit still, Deb jumped out of her chair and paced the room. Brian set a couple cups of hot coffee on the table and hunched over his, sipping it. "For Christ's sake, sit down. So Kelly's at Amy's. So what?"

"You don't understand. I think something's going on between them."

"Why don't you go and find out then?"

"I can't go there and find them together." Deb shrank from the thought. If she couldn't stand imagining it, how could she face the real thing?

"Call her and tell her how you feel."

"I can't," Deb said, stopping in her tracks. "It's probably too late anyway." The words started her walking again. "Where's the phone?"

The phone rang four times before Amy answered, which was when Deb hung up. Joining Brian at the table in the kitchen, she buried her head in her arms and cried.

"Call her back," he said, patting her on the shoulder. "Tell her not to do it."

"I can't. How can I? Goddamn it all to hell." She sobbed with renewed fervor.

"Here, drink this," Brian said, trying another tack. He poured Kahlua in the coffee cups and heated the mixture in the microwave.

"I suppose you think I deserve this," Deb said, taking a tentative sip.

"Well, you did sort of ask for it. You have to admit that." He lifted his cup to hers as if in a toast. "To the new year, may it be better than the old."

She took a long drink. "This does taste good."

Alone in Kathy's apartment, as they had been since Chris left them to meet someone New Year's Day, Marge and Kathy passed the afternoon watching football games. Not that Marge was crazy about the sport, as Kathy was, but they both were in football pools. An icy wind whipped newly fallen snow into a blinding white haze. Looking out the window made Marge shudder.

They lay on the floor eating microwave popcorn and making new bets to stimulate their interest. When Marge won a five dollar bet on which team would score first, she leaped to her feet and crowed, "And I don't even watch football!"

Playfully, Kathy tackled her and pinned her to the carpet. They stared at each other in sudden surprise. When Marge strained to free herself, Kathy bent over and kissed her.

It was up to Marge then. Had she resisted it would have ended, but she didn't. Kissing, they rolled on the floor, first one on top, then the other, and their kisses became deeper. The fumbling began. Soon, a gentle, exploratory hand between the legs was all that was necessary.

"Jesus," Marge said in alarmed surprise when they finally lay still, breathing heavily, and stared at each other from a distance of inches. "Holy cow. How did that happen?"

Kathy's face showed a mixture of fear and joy and astonishment. "I don't know. I'd say I was sorry but I'm not."

"You look scared." A scowl clouded Marge's face.

"I want to be friends still," Kathy said.

"We can be friends, but we can't do that again," Marge declared, turning away, denying that what had happened had been voluntary and vowing it would never happen again.

When Chris returned to join them for pizza and beer, she found Marge on the floor and Kathy curled up on a chair. "Well, guys, I met one handsome man today," she said, so caught up in relating her experiences she appeared to notice nothing out of the ordinary.

Marge pumped her with questions but hardly listened to the answers. Her confusion grew as she thought about the afternoon. Was she queer? She must be, because she had actually enjoyed doing it with Kathy. And now when she looked at Kathy, she remembered what it had been like with their hands and mouths on each other, and she felt the excitement anew. The best thing to do, she supposed, would be not to see Kathy until she sorted out her thoughts and feelings, and that, of course, had been what Kathy feared.

On the way back to their apartment, Chris froze Marge's insides with her words: "Ah ha, so you did it."

"What are you talking about?"

With a wicked grin Chris turned to Marge. "You know what I'm talking about. How'd you like it?"

"No, I don't know what you're talking about," Marge said indignantly and faced the window to hide from her sister.

"It's okay, Marge. I knew it would happen sooner or later."

"What the hell are you talking about, Chris? I'm not queer, if that's what you mean."

"I didn't say you were queer. I tried it once in college with a friend. We just cared for each other. I ran from it, too. I was always sorry about that, because I hurt her so much."

If Chris thought she would trap her into admitting anything, she had another thought coming. "I didn't do anything, and if you think that, I won't see Kathy anymore."

"Aw, come on, Marge. I thought you were through running from the truth," Chris said.

Marge stared out her side window at the white city. Mounds of snow marked the curbs, glistening in the street lights. Blown by strong winds, snow swirled and whipped around the car. Too bad the counselor she had seen was in Indiana. But Marge wasn't sure she could discuss this with anyone.

XIV

Early but always welcome, spring came to stay at the beginning of April. Grass had to be mowed, forsythia bloomed along with crocuses and daffodils and jonquils and hyacinths, magnolia trees and dogwoods. The budding branches of crabapples, redbuds, and lilacs nodded with the promise of flowers. Willows turned a yellowish green.

Amy greeted these signs of renewed life with unrestrained joy, so glad winter was over that she took to riding her bike to work. The business had been sold, the new managers were working with her and Ted. Ted planned to stay on after the transition. The auction of equipment not purchased with the rental would take place Saturday, and all week she and Ted had been transporting the machinery. Tomorrow she knew she'd have to spend the day at the auction.

Today was her last day at the rental, and, appreciating the sights and sounds and smells around her, she rode through the dew wet morning. She came upon an open woods in which spring beauties blanketed the ground, and she slowed as she passed them.

Next week she would fly to Mexico with Kelly. She hated missing any of spring and its brief beauty. But Kelly had planned the trip and surprised her with it last weekend. Don't plan my life, she had wanted to say, but she hadn't been able to disappoint Kelly.

All winter Amy had resisted Kelly's pleas for her to move into Kelly's apartment. But Amy had no intention of moving in with anyone again. During the past few months she had contemplated telling Kelly she only wanted to be friends, nothing more, but every time she started to say the words, Kelly had headed them off by telling her how much she cared for Amy.

Horn beeping, a Subaru sped past her and Amy raised a fist against the pounding of her heart. A hand waved through the sunroof as the car disappeared over the railroad tracks. Certain it was Deb, Amy shifted into a higher gear. She bounced over the tracks and noticed the car parked off the road in a nearby driveway with Deb leaning against its side.

Amy braked to a stop. "Scared the piss out of me, you know," she said to Deb.

"Sorry. I didn't want you swerving in front of me. I didn't recognize you until I passed." Deb looked young in the morning light, her green eyes shining and a crooked smile on her face.

"Where have you been all these months anyway?" Except for a brief thank you note, Amy had heard from Deb only when she called to see how she was, and after no return calls, she had stopped calling.

"Around. Keeping busy." The gold dove rested against Deb's skin where her blouse opened at the neck. She gazed into Amy's gray eyes which smiled back at her. It was still there, she marveled to herself, the magnetic attraction that drew her to Amy.

"It's been a long time since we saw each other. New Year's Day, wasn't it?" Amy's eyes focused momentarily on the pulse beating in Deb's neck.

"That's why I stopped. What are you doing Saturday?" Knowing she was setting herself up to be knocked down, she felt her face flush.

With regret Amy told her about the auction, that this was the last day for her at the rental. She said nothing about Mexico next week. "What are you doing Sunday?" she asked. If Deb could stick her neck out, so could she.

Deb was supposed to golf with friends Sunday. "Nothing. Want to do something?"

"Sure. What say I call you Saturday night? Will you be home?"

"Depends. Why don't we have dinner Saturday night?"

Amy hesitated. Kelly expected her after the auction.

"That's okay," Deb said quickly. "I forgot I had something planned Saturday night. Call me Sunday morning, if you can."

Amy watched Deb duck into the car and jerk the door shut. Nothing had changed for her, she realized. The pull toward Deb was still as strong as ever. Of its own volition her hand reached toward the vehicle as Deb put it in drive.

"Wait," she said. But the Subaru left her staring after it.

Deb had lived through torment when she was certain she had lost Amy to Kelly. Now she wasn't so sure Amy was completely out of reach. If Amy loved Kelly, they would live together. She watched Amy in the rearview mirror until the car topped a small rise and she lost sight of her.

Spring vacation would begin next week. Having to teach had saved her sanity during the winter months. Her energy had benefitted the students. After school she had prepared the next day's lectures and tests there instead of going home. Her classroom had become an after-school hangout for many students.

She had renewed old friendships and made new ones and spent many weekends skiing. She had seen all the new movies, read books, and combated the loneliness waiting in the wings for her few free hours.

After next week's spring break, she'd be coaching

track again. Maybe during the short vacation she could interest Amy in some fun — golfing or hiking or biking or something. Just when the students were getting to her, when she felt she could handle time alone — what did she do but let the person from whom she had run all winter back in her life. If nothing came of seeing Amy, she'd be where she had been at the beginning of January and have to handle that anguish all over again.

The auction was scheduled to begin at ten a.m., but Amy arrived early in case buyers had questions. Many of the pieces of equipment, parked in rows behind the auction warehouse, were like old friends to her, each one with a history. She had driven all the tractors, delivered and picked them up, worried about their condition, worked on them — changed their oil and fuel filters or spark plugs, greased their fittings, tightened and replaced parts. They had paid for themselves over the years and reaped a profit for her.

She wandered among them, answering buyers' questions and pointing out the special options and standard equipment: high/low ranges, power steering, live power take-offs, hydraulic three-point hitches, heaters on the diesels. Showing how easy it was to set them up and take them down, she cranked up a couple campers. She started a trencher and dug a short trench with it.

Then when the auctioneer commenced with his spiel, she followed him among the inventory and again pointed out positive selling points that might be overlooked by someone who was unfamiliar with the machinery. In the beginning he had turned to her, as the all-male crowd gathered around, and said in an amused condescending tone, "This little lady here will tell you all about this machinery." But halfway through the sale he stopped patronizing her, and it was her turn to be amused. This was how men had reacted to her knowledge all through the years at the rental.

When she drove away from the warehouse, for the first time she really felt that her slate was wiped clean, that she stood on the threshold of new experiences. Then she laughed deprecatingly at herself. There was nothing exciting or even worthwhile about her life.

When she unlocked Kelly's door, depression had settled over her like a blanket. Here she was in her mid-forties with nothing to show for it.

"How are you, honey?" Kelly asked, taking Amy in her arms.

Amy winced, as she always did when Kelly called her affectionate names, and moved out of the embrace. She plopped into a chair and ran a hand over her face. "Well, it's over. You know what I'd like to do right now with what's left of the day?"

"No, what?" Kelly asked, emerging from the kitchen and handing a drink to Amy.

Amy set it on the table next to her. She didn't want a drink. "I'd like to get Grit and go for a walk at Eagle Creek. Look at this day. It's gorgeous."

"We could sit on the balcony," Kelly suggested.

"I don't want to sit. Selling some of that stuff was like selling myself."

"We can go for a walk," Kelly said, missing the point.

Was there a point? "I'm sorry, but I want to go alone. Do you mind terribly?"

"Yes, I do. I waited all day to see you. Are you packed yet?"

"Packed? Oh, you mean for Mexico. No."

"You don't want to go, do you?"

"Sure I do, but I wish you'd consulted me before you bought tickets and made reservations."

Kelly studied her drink and then raised her eyes to meet Amy's disturbed gaze. "Can we just go and have a good time?"

"I can't really afford to go," Amy said.

"I'm paying," Kelly reminded her, an edge of impatience in her voice.

Shaking her head, Amy said, "I can't let you do that, Kelly." She sighed deeply. She started to tell Kelly what she should have told her months ago. Again she couldn't say the words. "I really do want to go for a walk with Grit. I'll call you later." She left knowing how much her leaving hurt Kelly.

No one was at John and Marilyn's house when she drove into the driveway. Grit cried deep in his throat greeting her which nearly made her cry. She left a note attached to the garage door where it couldn't be missed: *Took Grit for a run at Eagle Creek. Hope you don't mind.*

She and Grit made their way around the reservoir in the warm evening. She walked, while

Grit galloped ahead of her. Grit loved people, even kids, and he was well mannered. She stopped to talk to the people fishing, peering in their buckets to see if they had caught any fish. Ducks and geese and sandpipers populated the reservoir at this end. When she and Grit climbed the hill to the path through the woods, the turmoil that was her mind had settled down.

On the drive home she opened the windows for Grit, and he hung his head out one side, then the other; then he panted in her ear and licked her cheek. She reached back a hand and patted him once in a while. Before she had left John, she would have told the dog to sit and scolded him for licking her.

After taking Grit home, Amy drove to the apartment and took a shower. Showers always soothed her. Darkness fell while she was under the water. She thought she heard the phone ring, but she didn't answer it. If she had a serious conversation, she was afraid she might scream. She had to make decisions she didn't feel capable of making.

"Let's go to a movie and hit some of the hot spots," Chris suggested. "Saturday nights are meant to be fun, Marge."

"I suppose you mean Ken and you and me," Marge said. She was dressed in sweats and lay on her bed with a book.

"Ken has lots of friends who want to go out with you. All I have to do is give the word. Mike asks about you all the time. You met Mike." Chris applied make-up to her face, which didn't need it.

"I went out with Mike, remember? He reminds me of Matthew, and you know what Matthew was like. I don't need a repeat performance."

"Kathy called me yesterday at work. We're having lunch tomorrow. Would you like to come?"

"No, I wouldn't like to come." Marge still flushed darkly whenever Chris brought up Kathy's name.

"And you're still denying anything happened between you two," Chris said, pausing with mascara brush in hand to glance at Marge in the mirror.

"I don't have to deny anything. I'm going home next weekend, Chris. You want to come?"

"When did you decide to go home?" Chris asked, surprised.

"Just now."

"I'll see," Chris said, giving up on her sister. Let her stay home alone if that's what she wanted to do.

Marge had refused to see Kathy after New Year's Day. She had attempted to explain why to Kathy over the phone, but Kathy had insisted they could just be friends, and Marge had said that wasn't possible right then.

More miserable now than she had ever been, Marge sometimes thought she was losing it. It was Amy she wanted to see when she went home. David had told them at Christmas that Deb wasn't living with Amy anymore, that all Deb's clothes were gone from the apartment.

When Chris left with Ken, Marge would go to bed. As she had once exercised, now she sought escape in sleep.

But as soon as they were gone, someone knocked on the door.

Kathy stood in the entryway. "Mind if I come in for a few minutes? I was in the neighborhood."

"I told you I didn't want to see you for a while," Marge said, backing away.

"That was a long time ago, and I had to talk to you." She moved into the room and closed the door.

Marge retreated to the living room and settled on the floor. Kathy stared at her without saying anything.

"What is it?" Marge asked, impatient with the scrutiny.

"Nothing. I almost forgot what you look like."

"Well, that might have been better. Sit down. Can I get you anything?" But she didn't move to get up.

"Diet Coke or something, if you have it."

Marge rose in one fluid motion and fetched them each a drink, then crossed her feet and folded her body to the floor. "Talk," she commanded.

Kathy took a sip. "I'd like to be friends again. There's a good movie showing. Wouldn't you like to see it?"

"That's what you have to say?" Marge asked rudely.

"Yeah, that's about the extent of it," Kathy replied mildly, her eyebrows raised in question.

"I want to stay in tonight. I'm tired," Marge said in a flat voice.

Kathy's face reddened slightly. "You're cruel, Marge, you know that?"

"So I've been told before. I'll call you next time. Okay?" Marge rose to her feet again.

"Don't bother." Kathy set the can down with a decisive bang and stalked out of the apartment.

Marge went to bed and dreamed that her mother was making love to her. They were laughing and rolling, arms wrapped around each other, under flowering crab trees on fresh green grass. A soft warm breeze whispered over them. Her mother turned into Chris and then Marilyn before she struggled up out of the dream.

What the hell did that mean? she wondered, getting up to take a shower and rummage around the refrigerator for something to eat.

She called her mother.

"Marge?"

There was such astonishment in her mother's voice that she felt guilty for not calling until now. "How are you, Mom?"

"Good. And you?"

"I want to come home next weekend and wondered if I could stay with you."

"I'd love to have you here, honey, but I'm supposed to be in Mexico next weekend."

"Oh." Disappointment was obvious in that one small word.

"Maybe I won't go," Amy said quickly.

"Don't do that for me, Mom." Touched, Marge refused what she thought was above and beyond motherliness. "I'll come the weekend after, if that's all right."

"That's wonderful. Is everything okay? You sound kind of down."

"I'm fine. Really. I'm just spending the evening reading." Lieface, she thought. She'd been deep in sleep.

Knowing Deb slept late weekends, Amy didn't call her until nine the next morning. She couldn't remember who was supposed to call whom, but she was wide awake at seven, had read the paper by eight, and was now showered and ready to go anywhere.

Showing up at Amy's door dressed in shorts and sneakers half an hour later, Amy took one look at Deb and said, "Let me guess. We're going to hike somewhere. Right?"

"You're clever today. But we're going to rent a canoe and go down Sugar Creek."

Surrounded by sheer tree-studded bluffs through which the stream had cut a chute, the water rippled over jutting rocks, sometimes flowing swiftly enough to be considered rapids. Wide rocks and occasional sandy spots along the banks offered places to stop and rest. The creek was high and propelled the craft along. Several times they ground over big rocks just under the surface and spun around to find themselves going downstream backwards. They got caught under a dead tree hanging over a corner of the creek and Amy was dumped unceremoniously into the cold water. After that, they landed and sat on one of the huge flat rocks and ate deli and drank wine.

"What a good idea this was. I don't know why I never think to do this," Amy said.

Deb grinned at her. "You look like a wet noodle."

Amy ran her fingers through her tangled hair. She had been shivering, but the heat of the sun now warmed her through her wet clothes. She felt like she was steaming.

"You know, I've got vacation this week," Deb said. "Would you like to do some things, since you don't have to work anymore, or have you got a job already?"

Shit, Amy thought, why was she going to Mexico? She chewed on her lower lip.

"It's all right, Amy. We don't have to do anything. Shall we go?" Deb jumped to her feet and brushed off the seat of her shorts.

"Just sit down, will you? I'd like more wine."

Deb hesitated and then squatted down to pour them both another plastic cup of wine.

"I'd love to do things with you next week, but I've got to go to Mexico." Her eyes worriedly searched Deb's face.

Snorting with disbelief, Deb said, "You don't want to go to Mexico, woman? I'd love to go."

"Well, just not next week," Amy said rather dejectedly. "First Marge calls and wants to visit next weekend. Then you have time off and want to do some things." Amy lay back on the rock and watched Deb from under an arm.

Sitting down, Deb wrapped her arms around her

legs and rested her chin on her knees. Was there a conspiracy against the two of them getting together, even for fun?

"Would you like to come?" Amy asked, wondering what she would say to Kelly if Deb said yes.

"Who are you going with?" Deb asked casually.

"Kelly surprised me with this trip. It wasn't my idea," Amy explained, still watching Deb, noticing her back stiffening.

"How nice," Deb said between clenched teeth. She couldn't afford to compete this way. "How was the auction?" she asked. "And how is Marge?"

"The auction went well, and Marge sounded a little down but she didn't say why. Deb . . ." Amy sat up so she could look into Deb's face. "For what it's worth I'd rather spend next week with you, and you didn't answer my question about going to Mexico with us."

For a fleeting moment Deb let her guard drop, and she felt exposed. Then she covered up. "I'm sure Kelly would be delighted if I came along," she said with heavy sarcasm. "Where are you going anyway?"

"An island off the Yucatán Peninsula. Near Cancun."

"What day are you going?"

"Monday."

"Well, we better get you home so you can pack."

"I'm in no hurry to get home. I'm having a wonderful day."

Dropping Amy off at her apartment, Deb refused to come in even for a few minutes. "You have to get ready for your trip."

Stepping out of the car, Amy bent down and talked through the open car door. "Let's get together again. Okay?"

"Sure," Deb replied. What on earth for? Goddamn sucking world, she thought. But a kernel of hope formed at Amy's suggestion. Maybe it would be another beginning; maybe today had been just that.

Amy stopped in at Kelly's bookstore the next afternoon. She had slept little the previous night, because of what she planned to say to Kelly today. "Can we talk alone?" she asked her.

"Sure. Let's go upstairs."

Amy blurted out what she had to say as if she were afraid Kelly might change her mind. "I can't go to Mexico, Kelly. It just wouldn't be right. Maybe you can take Barbara or someone else with you."

They stood at an open window in the empty room where Sheila had spoken to the women's group months ago. Amy's heart thudded in her chest, but this time she was determined to hold her own.

Kelly dropped her eyes to her hands resting on the windowsill. She pursed her lips and nodded. "Okay."

Amy went limp, her resolve no longer needed. "You don't mind?"

"Would it matter?" Kelly gave her a sad smile.

Amy shook her head. "I'm sorry."

Shrugging, Kelly said, "I know, Amy. It was fun but it wasn't going anywhere, was it?"

"No."

Kelly raised her eyebrows. "Friends?"

"I'd like that," Amy said, smiling shakily.

XV

Lying in what must have been Deb's room, Marge wondered about the furniture. It didn't look familiar and she didn't think it was new. Was it Deb's? Anyway, had Deb slept here or in the double bed with her mother?

She had arrived an hour ago, eaten a sandwich, and told Amy she was tired. So they had both gone to bed. Marge knew her mother was curious to know why she was here and not at her father's. She felt sleep moving in on her, muddying the edges of her mind. Unresisting, she yielded to it.

The cat wound around Amy's legs, a low guttural purr escaping from its throat, sounding like a distant car. Amy picked Briny up and held her while she read the Saturday morning paper and waited for Marge to make her appearance.

She had to use the bathroom but knew Marge was in there and didn't want to intrude on her. A few years ago she wouldn't have hesitated to barge in while either of the girls was in the bathroom. Now she was wary of infringing on Marge's privacy, afraid of her resentment. Amy trod carefully around her daughters, fearful they might snap at her. It was a new experience for her, she who had been so close to her children, to carefully avoid their imagined displeasure where once she would have jumped in with her advice and opinions.

"How about some breakfast?" she asked Marge, who had just entered the sun drenched living room in shorts and T-shirt.

"Sure. I'm starved."

"Just a minute. I've got to use the john and then I'll fix us something." Amy, still holding Briny, dumped her unceremoniously on the floor, and the cat meowed plaintively.

"What's wrong, Briny?" Marge scooped the cat up and carried her to the patio door. A soft breeze blew in the screen and caressed them. "What a day," she whispered, her face in the cat's fur, hearing and feeling the deep purr. The claws kneaded her arm and she had to set Briny down to protect her skin. "How can you hold her? Her claws are like needles."

"I know. She needs to be declawed," Amy agreed, coming down the hall and rounding the corner to the kitchen.

"Isn't that cruel?"

"Not really. It keeps her out of trees, too. Makes her a less efficient bird catcher."

"Can I help?" Marge appeared in the doorway.

"Sure, you can cut up the veggies."

"Mom?"

"Hmmm?"

"Where's Deb?"

"Living with her mother. Why?" Alert, Amy waited tensely for the next question.

"You know Kathy?"

"Yes, what about her?" Amy asked.

"Well, she's gay, you know."

"I know," Amy replied quietly, her back turned to her daughter.

Marge cast around for the right words without being too specific. "Well, she's got a thing for me. You know, she likes me that way, and I haven't seen her since New Year's because of it and I feel mean about it."

"I can understand that."

"What?"

"That you feel mean about it. You can be just friends, you know. One thing I found out about gay people is that they're just people, like you and me. They're no threat to anyone. I think most gay women are more inhibited than straight women." Amy paused and took a deep breath. She still didn't look at Marge because she felt, and rightly, that Marge didn't want to be scrutinized.

"Do you think it runs in families?"

"Being gay, you mean?" For some reason, perhaps because she was nervous, Amy wanted desperately to laugh. She glanced at her daughter for the first time and caught Marge's nod. "I don't know. For years I was homophobic, which was stupid. A lot of gay women are so deep in the closet their worst nightmares are being exposed as lesbians."

A long silence followed this statement. Amy sauteed the vegetables Marge had diced, then mixed in whipped egg whites and added shredded cheese.

"I never thought I'd have this conversation with you. I never thought I'd forgive you for leaving Dad. Are you sorry you left?" Marge's voice came out low and unsteady.

Thoughtfully, Amy shook her head. "I never thought you'd talk about it either. And no, I'm not sorry. I might be if your dad wasn't happy, but he is. I'm not crazy about myself right now, but it's not because I left."

Marge asked the obvious question. "Why then?"

"I just sort of screwed things up. Sometimes I think things happen for a purpose but most of the time I think we just bumble along, making mistakes as we go."

"What mistakes? Deb?" Now that the ice was broken Marge wanted to know.

"It's too complicated to explain, Marge, but Deb wasn't a mistake. She should still be here."

Marge, looking at the floor, noticed a tiny dark spot on the linoleum and rubbed it with her toe. "I hated her, you know. If it hadn't been for her, you'd still be at home."

"I know how you felt, and I understand, but it was more my doing than hers. Don't be afraid of Kathy. I doubt she'd make a move without encouragement. You can be her friend."

Marge didn't reply. But she thought she'd call

Kathy when she returned to Milwaukee, maybe make amends or try to. She still needed time to sort through her emotions over Kathy.

"What do you want to do today?" Amy asked after breakfast.

"Let's go to Brown County."

"To the park? To the town?"

"Both."

"Have you called your dad?"

"Not yet. I'll do it now."

For some reason, Amy felt a surge of joy because Marge hadn't called John until then.

Sunday, after Marge left for Milwaukee, Amy dialed Deb's number. She hadn't talked to Deb since the canoe trip down Sugar Creek, and she was nervous. "I would have called earlier but Marge was here this weekend."

"How is she?"

"Confused."

Deb uttered a low laugh. "Aren't we all?"

"But she talked to me, Deb, about us, about Kathy — remember Kathy?"

"From the bike ride?"

"Yes. Kathy's got a thing for Marge, and Marge doesn't know how to handle it, I guess."

"Well, I'm not surprised." Deb said questioningly, "I saw Kelly with Barbara this Saturday."

"Yes. They're getting back together, I think." What to say now? "Look, you want to do something next weekend if the weather's good?"

"There's a sailboat exhibit at Glendale this week. I'm going tomorrow night. Would you like to go?" Deb asked in a rush.

"That might be fun. You still want a sailboat?"

"Sure do. What time do you want me to pick you up?"

"Want to eat out first?"

"I'd like that."

The next night Deb arrived at Amy's apartment while Amy watched national news on television. They watched the rest of the news, then went out into the warm, sweet smelling early May evening.

On the way to dinner, Deb said, "You told me Marge talked about us. What did she say?"

"Not a whole lot. She wanted to know if I was sorry I left John, presumably because you were gone."

"Because I was gone?"

"Because we weren't together anymore, you and me."

"Are you? Sorry about leaving John, I mean."

"No, I'm not. I did what I had to do at the time. I'm sorry I hurt everyone, but it was the right thing for me."

"Does she still hate me? That bothered me a lot, the way your kids blamed me."

Amy shrugged. "I don't know if she hates you anymore. It bothered me, too, their blaming you." She couldn't help Deb with her guilt. She had enough of her own. "I told her it was my fault more than yours."

"Did you?" Deb threw Amy an interested glance.

They were seated immediately in the Forum and ordered wine while they studied the menu.

"Hey, girls, how are you two?" Brian descended on them. "I was passing by and saw you in the window."

They grinned at him in welcome. "Join us,

Brian." Amy patted the bench, and he slid in next to her.

"I'll have a drink with you broads and then I have to go. I'm supposed to meet Douglas at St. V's and go on to more exciting places."

"Things are working out for you two?" Deb asked.

"Probably about as well as they are for you two."

Deb and Amy exchanged a look. What did that mean?

Brian said, "We're sort of stalking around each other, occasionally wagging our tails, like a couple of dogs."

Amy laughed loudly. "Jesus, what a comparison."

When Brian left, they both ordered another glass of wine. Deb twirled the stem of her wine glass and picked up the thread of their unfinished discussion. "To say it was somebody's fault is to imply it was wrong."

"Well, it was to the kids. They thought John and I had a good marriage. I spent all those years trying to be a good example, and then I walked out on my family."

"I've wondered if that's why we didn't make a go of it."

"What?" Amy stared with troubled eyes at Deb.

"Did you think you had a good marriage?"

The question required some thought. "I think I thought I did. It wasn't all that bad, you know." She spoke slowly. "You brought something out in me I didn't know was there."

"We tried to build without dealing with their hurt or our guilt."

"That's not why you fooled around with Jane," Amy said suddenly.

"Maybe it is."

"Shit," was Amy's disbelieving comment.

The waitress brought their salads and they stopped talking until she left. "But you're right about the guilt. I think I'll always feel guilty about hurting them," Amy remarked.

The sailboats filled the mall with brightly colored sails, their masts reaching toward the skylights. The two women stood in the entry hallway in awe. Amy trailed Deb, who walked among the boats until she found a Sunfish.

She loved the rainbow hues of the sail. "This is the one I want, Amy. I'd like to put this on Eagle Creek. We could have such fun this summer," she said, including Amy with the impulsively spoken words.

"I'll have time this summer," Amy remarked, her smile hesitant. She would make time.

Deb dickered with the salesman and Amy listened in the background, surprised when she realized Deb was serious, that she really was going to buy a Sunfish.

On their way out of the mall, Deb — dazed by what she considered a rash act — said to Amy, "I actually bought it. Will you help me pick it up after the show ends Saturday?"

"Sure."

"If it's nice out, we can sail Sunday," she said with growing excitement. "I'll have to get a hitch put on my car and have it wired, get a couple boat cushions before the weekend," she thought aloud. "I can't believe I did this."

"Neither can I," Amy said with a laugh, "but I think it's great."

* * * * *

Amy drove home after shopping the following morning. Rain threatened: lightning flashed across the clouded sky and thunder rumbled in the wake of the sudden glare of light. In the quiet before the storm, Amy parked, picked up her mail and hurried into the building. She warmed a cup of coffee and paged through the classified section of the *Indianapolis Star*. There was a help wanted ad from the business she had sold. Should she offer her services? She certainly was qualified. Putting the paper down, she stared out the window at the sheets of rain pelting the patio glass door.

What to do with her life? She had to admit she was sometimes bored with her free days, but there was enough money. The settlement from selling the house and the rental business, after investing, would support her in a modest way. However, when she was confined to the apartment on days like this, she became restless. Until now she'd had little time to contemplate her life — past, present, or future. Perhaps it was better not to do so.

She called the rental number and Ted answered. "How's it going?" she asked him.

"Good. How'd you like to work for me? I'm the new manager."

"I'll give it some serious thought." And she would. "What's new there?"

"Can't stay away, huh? There's a lot of new, neat equipment. You ought to come in and see it."

"I will when it stops raining."

"Got to go. Here comes a customer."

The day stretched out in front of her like an

empty page. Why not enjoy it while she could? It looked like she'd be working again before long, but she promised herself she wouldn't work weekends.

Deb and Amy launched the sailboat Sunday morning early. The day, already hot and windy, was just what they wanted, except it was still a little early in the season to be dumped in the water. They had to ask for help to rig the boat right but when it was done, the wind caught the brightly colored sail and propelled the Sunfish across the water at breakneck speed.

Deb handed Amy the sheet and told her when to haul it in and when to let it out. "Lean back," Deb yelled as the boat heeled and water raced across the deck, some of it leaking into the cockpit. They sat, side by side, feet braced against the opposite side of the boat.

The next thing Amy knew they were flung out of the craft into the sail which was sinking in the blue depths. She heard herself shriek and Deb laugh. The icy water took their breath away and they struggled to right the boat and clamber back in.

"What a christening, huh?" Deb said, holding one side while Amy pulled herself over the other, then joining her once again in the sailboat.

After turning over what seemed numberless times, they were exhausted from righting the boat and hauling themselves back into it. "I had no idea this was so much fun," Amy commented, leaning back next to Deb against the wind in the sail, their heads skimming the water.

"It's not usually this windy. I can't remember it being this much fun."

Their faces were inches apart and they grinned at each other. The Sunfish stood on its side close to the point of no return, when it would be too late to bring it back.

Amy's voice rose to a shout. "Here we go again."

It was past six when they loaded the boat on the trailer and Deb took Amy home. "Now I understand," Amy said, a pleasant tiredness sapping her.

"What do you understand?" Deb asked.

"Why you wanted a sailboat. Want to order a pizza from my place?"

Regret tugged at Deb. "I'd love to, but I promised Mom I'd be there for dinner, and I'm going to be late as it is. I could call and beg off, I suppose, but it's a party and she needs my help."

"Oh, you go. I think I'll just shower and go to bed and read anyway." The more time she spent with Deb the more she hated telling her goodbye.

Deb would have liked to get into Amy's bed with her, but it didn't look like it was ever going to happen. The more they were together, the better friends they became and romance didn't fit in. "Next weekend?" she asked, when Amy got out of the car.

"Love to," Amy replied.

Toward the end of the week spring forgot itself. Temperatures dipped into the low sixties and a cool northwesterly wind brought cold rain. Saturday was out for sailing. And when Sunday morning dawned under glowering clouds, Deb lay in bed in a state of depression and stared out the window. She had sacrificed the past week to students, and she desperately wanted this day to herself and Amy. If they didn't sail, what would they do with it? She decided to tow the boat to Amy's anyway. Maybe the sun would come out later.

When she arrived, Amy was drinking coffee and reading the paper. "I didn't expect you so early. Come on in. Rotten out, isn't it?"

"I brought the boat, but I don't think it'd be much fun sailing today."

"Cup of coffee?"

"Sure. Want to do something else?" Deb followed Amy into the kitchen.

"Like what?" Amy turned to face her, coffee pot in one hand, cup in the other.

Without thinking, as if it were the most natural thing in the world, Deb leaned forward and kissed Amy's cheek. Feeling the softness of the skin beneath her lips, she continued the kiss to Amy's eyes, to her nose, back to her cheek and neck and finally her mouth. Deb's heart pounded, her face flushed. She took Amy's face between her hands, unwilling to end the kiss, thrilled she was actually doing this.

Amy set the coffee pot down but still held the cup in her other hand. There was no place within reach to put it. She grabbed Deb and pulled her close, her eyes open. Feeling Deb's tongue, she touched it with her own. Her breathing became ragged to match her rapidly beating heart. She forgot the coffee cup and it fell to the floor.

They jumped away at the sound. "Shit," Amy said.

"Sorry," Deb responded, but she wasn't sorry. She was enraptured. "Where's the broom?"

"Where it always was," Amy replied. "Forget it."

"No, I'll clean it up."

Together they swept the shards into the dustpan — Deb wielding the broom, Amy holding the dustpan. Dumping the broken pieces in the wastebasket, Amy met Deb's eyes. A smile stole across her face. "Want your coffee now?"

"I want you," Deb said in a choked voice.

"Well?" Amy raised her eyebrows. "Here I am."

There was an awkward moment when they stared at each other. Then Deb took Amy's hand and drew her down the hall to the bedroom, where they stood beside the bed just looking at each other for what seemed a long time.

Deb ran her hands up Amy's arms to her shoulders and back down again. Amy rested her hands tentatively on Deb's waist. Almost in slow motion they leaned toward each other and kissed, hesitantly at first, then deeper — tongues flickering around the insides of their lips. Again they backed off and looked at each other, laughing a little to ease the tension.

"Take it off," Deb whispered, sliding her hands up under Amy's shirt, smiling when she felt no bra.

Sucking air, fingers fumbling, Amy unbuttoned Deb's shirt. "You take it off," she demanded in a soft, urgent voice. "Now."

Amy pulled her T-shirt off with one quick motion, and Deb shrugged out of her shirt. Then they paused once more to look at each other. Amy reached behind her and took the phone off the hook, dropping the receiver onto the floor. She felt Deb's hands on her, caressing her breasts, her nipples. "You take my breath away, you know it," she said in a low, rough voice.

"That's what you do to me," Deb replied.

Deb was now reaching inside Amy's sweats, and Amy grabbed her and threw herself and Deb unceremoniously onto the bed, briefly gaining the upper hand. Lying on top of Deb, she grinned down at her. "Got you."

"Oh no, you don't." With effort, Deb rolled the two of them until she was on top. Her hand slipped inside the band of Amy's sweatpants, tugging at them.

They dropped the rest of their clothes off the side of the bed and just held each other. "I could spend the rest of the day like this," Deb said, but her hands were busy again, moving between Amy's legs, fingers gently probing.

Amy's breathing changed to shallow, quick gasps, and she wondered why it was only Deb's touch that did this to her. If Deb were clumsy, would she still react this way to her? She thought maybe she would.

"Why are you smiling?" Deb asked, looking down at her.

"It's nice to see you in your lovemaking pose again. I thought maybe I never would."

In reply Deb kissed Amy's mouth, her neck, her breasts while her fingers moved in a slowly quickening rhythm.

Hugging Deb to her, Amy lay quiet for the space of a few minutes, then pushed Deb onto her back. But she was suddenly reluctant to begin what she had once enjoyed so much.

A heaviness weighed her down and she was strangely averse to commit herself. Briefly, she recalled the many ways Deb had hurt her in the past year, chalk marks against the woman who now responded enthusiastically to her touch. This same woman who had turned her away more than a few times and then had taken someone else in her place. Amy felt she could just as easily lie down and sleep as raise herself to perform the act of love. Was that what it was — love? Resting her head in one hand, she caressed Deb with the other.

"Why do you look like that?" Deb asked, elevating her hips slightly as Amy's hand paused between her legs.

"Like what?"

"Like your mind is somewhere else."

"It's here all right." Amy put her thoughts away. What was the point? she asked herself. She loved this woman. She bent to kiss Deb and, using her mouth and hands, prolonged the lovemaking with a skill acquired through sensitivity and practice. She didn't see Deb succumb to the passion she evoked, but she heard her response and smiled.

A spring wind howled around the building, spattering intermittent rain at it. The blinds were closed against the outside world. A light glowed warmly next to the bed where they lay intertwined most of the day, making love, finding new ways to make love, and laughing at their ingenuity. Once they fell asleep with lips touching at the start of an embrace. Toward evening they arose and rummaged around the kitchen.

"Are you moving back in? Your furniture is still here."

"If you want me to, I will." Deb approached Amy from behind, enclosed her in an embrace and buried her face in Amy's neck.

Amy pressed her cheek against Deb's hair. "I do."

Deb said, "Aren't your kids coming home for Memorial Day?"

"Mmm hmm. Why?"

"Wouldn't it be better to wait until they leave?"

"Probably. Do you want to wait?"

"Do you want me to?"

"There you go, answering a question with a question."

"It's up to you, Amy. They're your kids."

"I don't want you to wait. Let's move you this week sometime."

Epilogue

Leaning on the counter, Amy filled out a contract for a customer. She had worked mornings at the rental for nearly a year now. Mornings were the busy times and when she wasn't at the counter, she was in the office doing book work.

Outside the window she saw Deb pull into the parking lot with the O'Day in tow behind Amy's Grand Am. They had purchased the bigger sailboat last fall. They talked of buying an even larger boat and taking it on the Great Lakes, maybe even the ocean, but so far it was just talk.

"I'm leaving," she said to Ted, when the customer departed with a lawnmower. "Is someone coming in to take my place?"

"At one. Go ahead. It's quiet today."

"Hi, babe," Deb greeted her as Amy climbed into the car.

"Hello, sweetie. It's so nice to be able to walk out of that place and forget everything. I never thought I could do that. Out of sight, out of mind. What did you do all morning?"

"Answered the phone."

"Who called?"

"Chris woke me at seven-thirty. You just missed her. She and Marge and Kathy are driving home Memorial Day weekend. David is coming, too."

Amy tensed. Her kids still hadn't really accepted Deb. Amy wondered if they ever would, but at least they spoke to Deb when she answered the phone. Their refusal to fully acknowledge Deb's place in Amy's life had caused friction between Deb and Amy more than once, but there was nothing Amy could do except hope time would mellow their attitude toward Deb. "Who else?"

"Brian woke me at eight, wanting to know if we could all go sailing next weekend."

"Who's we all?" Thinking of Brian always made Amy smile.

"He and Douglas and you and me. Is the boat big enough?"

"Barely," Amy said. "Let's hope for calm. I can't believe they're still together."

"I can't either. They even argue about folding the laundry. Then Marilyn called at eight-twenty just to talk. We, mostly she, talked until after nine. By then I was wide awake, of course."

"Those were all the calls?"

"Weren't those enough?"

Amy reached across the space between them and took Deb's hand, locking fingers. "It's good to see you."

Deb replied by squeezing Amy's hand. "We have an anniversary coming up. Remember?"

"How could I forget? How do you want to spend it?"

"In bed, the same way we spent it last year." She turned toward Amy.

"Sounds good to me," Amy replied, smiling.

"Pretty day, isn't it?" Deb commented.

"Gorgeous," Amy agreed. "Aren't we lucky."

A few of the publications of

THE NAIAD PRESS, INC.

P.O. Box 10543 • Tallahassee, Florida 32302

Phone (904) 539-5965

Mail orders welcome. Please include 15% postage.

ZETA BASE by Judith Alguire. 208 pp. Lesbian triangle on a future Earth.	ISBN 0-941483-94-0	$9.95
SECOND CHANCE by Jackie Calhoun. 256 pp. Contemporary Lesbian lives and loves.	ISBN 0-941483-93-2	9.95
MURDER BY TRADITION by Katherine V. Forrest. 288 pp. A Kate Delafield Mystery. 4th in a series.	ISBN 0-941483-89-4	18.95
BENEDICTION by Diane Salvatore. 272 pp. Striking, contemporary romantic novel.	ISBN 0-941483-90-8	9.95
CALLING RAIN by Karen Marie Christa Minns. 240 pp. Spellbinding, erotic love story	ISBN 0-941483-87-8	9.95
BLACK IRIS by Jeane Harris. 192 pp. Caroline's hidden past . . .	ISBN 0-941483-68-1	8.95
TOUCHWOOD by Karin Kallmaker. 240 pp. Loving, May/December romance.	ISBN 0-941483-76-2	8.95
BAYOU CITY SECRETS by Deborah Powell. 224 pp. A Hollis Carpenter mystery. First in a series.	ISBN 0-941483-91-6	8.95
COP OUT by Claire McNab. 208 pp. 4th Det. Insp. Carol Ashton mystery.	ISBN 0-941483-84-3	8.95
LODESTAR by Phyllis Horn. 224 pp. Romantic, fast-moving adventure.	ISBN 0-941483-83-5	8.95
THE BEVERLY MALIBU by Katherine V. Forrest. 288 pp. A Kate Delafield Mystery. 3rd in a series. (HC)	ISBN 0-941483-47-9	16.95
Paperback	ISBN 0-941483-48-7	9.95
THAT OLD STUDEBAKER by Lee Lynch. 272 pp. Andy's affair with Regina and her attachment to her beloved car.	ISBN 0-941483-82-7	9.95
PASSION'S LEGACY by Lori Paige. 224 pp. Sarah is swept into the arms of Augusta Pym in this delightful historical romance.	ISBN 0-941483-81-9	8.95
THE PROVIDENCE FILE by Amanda Kyle Williams. 256 pp. Second espionage thriller featuring lesbian agent Madison McGuire	ISBN 0-941483-92-4	8.95
I LEFT MY HEART by Jaye Maiman. 320 pp. A Robin Miller Mystery. First in a series.	ISBN 0-941483-72-X	9.95

THE PRICE OF SALT by Patricia Highsmith (writing as Claire Morgan). 288 pp. Classic lesbian novel, first issued in 1952 . . . acknowledged by its author under her own, very famous, name. ISBN 1-56280-003-5 8.95

SIDE BY SIDE by Isabel Miller. 256 pp. From beloved author of *Patience and Sarah.* ISBN 0-941483-77-0 8.95

SOUTHBOUND by Sheila Ortiz Taylor. 240 pp. Hilarious sequel to *Faultline.* ISBN 0-941483-78-9 8.95

STAYING POWER: LONG TERM LESBIAN COUPLES by Susan E. Johnson. 352 pp. Joys of coupledom. ISBN 0-941-483-75-4 12.95

SLICK by Camarin Grae. 304 pp. Exotic, erotic adventure. ISBN 0-941483-74-6 9.95

NINTH LIFE by Lauren Wright Douglas. 256 pp. A Caitlin Reece mystery. 2nd in a series. ISBN 0-941483-50-9 8.95

PLAYERS by Robbi Sommers. 192 pp. Sizzling, erotic novel. ISBN 0-941483-73-8 8.95

MURDER AT RED ROOK RANCH by Dorothy Tell. 224 pp. First Poppy Dillworth adventure. ISBN 0-941483-80-0 8.95

LESBIAN SURVIVAL MANUAL by Rhonda Dicksion. 112 pp. Cartoons! ISBN 0-941483-71-1 8.95

A ROOM FULL OF WOMEN by Elisabeth Nonas. 256 pp. Contemporary Lesbian lives. ISBN 0-941483-69-X 8.95

MURDER IS RELATIVE by Karen Saum. 256 pp. The first Brigid Donovan mystery. ISBN 0-941483-70-3 8.95

PRIORITIES by Lynda Lyons 288 pp. Science fiction with a twist. ISBN 0-941483-66-5 8.95

THEME FOR DIVERSE INSTRUMENTS by Jane Rule. 208 pp. Powerful romantic lesbian stories. ISBN 0-941483-63-0 8.95

LESBIAN QUERIES by Hertz & Ertman. 112 pp. The questions you were too embarrassed to ask. ISBN 0-941483-67-3 8.95

CLUB 12 by Amanda Kyle Williams. 288 pp. Espionage thriller featuring a lesbian agent! ISBN 0-941483-64-9 8.95

DEATH DOWN UNDER by Claire McNab. 240 pp. 3rd Det. Insp. Carol Ashton mystery. ISBN 0-941483-39-8 8.95

MONTANA FEATHERS by Penny Hayes. 256 pp. Vivian and Elizabeth find love in frontier Montana. ISBN 0-941483-61-4 8.95

CHESAPEAKE PROJECT by Phyllis Horn. 304 pp. Jessie & Meredith in perilous adventure. ISBN 0-941483-58-4 8.95

LIFESTYLES by Jackie Calhoun. 224 pp. Contemporary Lesbian lives and loves. ISBN 0-941483-57-6 8.95

VIRAGO by Karen Marie Christa Minns. 208 pp. Darsen has chosen Ginny.	ISBN 0-941483-56-8	8.95
WILDERNESS TREK by Dorothy Tell. 192 pp. Six women on vacation learning "new" skills.	ISBN 0-941483-60-6	8.95
MURDER BY THE BOOK by Pat Welch. 256 pp. A Helen Black Mystery. First in a series.	ISBN 0-941483-59-2	8.95
BERRIGAN by Vicki P. McConnell. 176 pp. Youthful Lesbian — romantic, idealistic Berrigan.	ISBN 0-941483-55-X	8.95
LESBIANS IN GERMANY by Lillian Faderman & B. Eriksson. 128 pp. Fiction, poetry, essays.	ISBN 0-941483-62-2	8.95
THERE'S SOMETHING I'VE BEEN MEANING TO TELL YOU Ed. by Loralee MacPike. 288 pp. Gay men and lesbians coming out to their children.	ISBN 0-941483-44-4	9.95
	ISBN 0-941483-54-1	16.95
LIFTING BELLY by Gertrude Stein. Ed. by Rebecca Mark. 104 pp. Erotic poetry.	ISBN 0-941483-51-7	8.95
	ISBN 0-941483-53-3	14.95
ROSE PENSKI by Roz Perry. 192 pp. Adult lovers in a long-term relationship.	ISBN 0-941483-37-1	8.95
AFTER THE FIRE by Jane Rule. 256 pp. Warm, human novel by this incomparable author.	ISBN 0-941483-45-2	8.95
SUE SLATE, PRIVATE EYE by Lee Lynch. 176 pp. The gay folk of Peacock Alley are *all cats.*	ISBN 0-941483-52-5	8.95
CHRIS by Randy Salem. 224 pp. Golden oldie. Handsome Chris and her adventures.	ISBN 0-941483-42-8	8.95
THREE WOMEN by March Hastings. 232 pp. Golden oldie. A triangle among wealthy sophisticates.	ISBN 0-941483-43-6	8.95
RICE AND BEANS by Valeria Taylor. 232 pp. Love and romance on poverty row.	ISBN 0-941483-41-X	8.95
PLEASURES by Robbi Sommers. 204 pp. Unprecedented eroticism.	ISBN 0-941483-49-5	8.95
EDGEWISE by Camarin Grae. 372 pp. Spellbinding adventure.	ISBN 0-941483-19-3	9.95
FATAL REUNION by Claire McNab. 224 pp. 2nd Det. Inspec. Carol Ashton mystery.	ISBN 0-941483-40-1	8.95
KEEP TO ME STRANGER by Sarah Aldridge. 372 pp. Romance set in a department store dynasty.	ISBN 0-941483-38-X	9.95
HEARTSCAPE by Sue Gambill. 204 pp. American lesbian in Portugal.	ISBN 0-941483-33-9	8.95
IN THE BLOOD by Lauren Wright Douglas. 252 pp. Lesbian science fiction adventure fantasy	ISBN 0-941483-22-3	8.95

THE BEE'S KISS by Shirley Verel. 216 pp. Delicate, delicious romance. ISBN 0-941483-36-3 8.95

RAGING MOTHER MOUNTAIN by Pat Emmerson. 264 pp. Furosa Firechild's adventures in Wonderland. ISBN 0-941483-35-5 8.95

IN EVERY PORT by Karin Kallmaker. 228 pp. Jessica's sexy, adventuresome travels. ISBN 0-941483-37-7 8.95

OF LOVE AND GLORY by Evelyn Kennedy. 192 pp. Exciting WWII romance. ISBN 0-941483-32-0 8.95

CLICKING STONES by Nancy Tyler Glenn. 288 pp. Love transcending time. ISBN 0-941483-31-2 9.95

SURVIVING SISTERS by Gail Pass. 252 pp. Powerful love story. ISBN 0-941483-16-9 8.95

SOUTH OF THE LINE by Catherine Ennis. 216 pp. Civil War adventure. ISBN 0-941483-29-0 8.95

WOMAN PLUS WOMAN by Dolores Klaich. 300 pp. Supurb Lesbian overview. ISBN 0-941483-28-2 9.95

SLOW DANCING AT MISS POLLY'S by Sheila Ortiz Taylor. 96 pp. Lesbian Poetry ISBN 0-941483-30-4 7.95

DOUBLE DAUGHTER by Vicki P. McConnell. 216 pp. A Nyla Wade Mystery, third in the series. ISBN 0-941483-26-6 8.95

HEAVY GILT by Delores Klaich. 192 pp. Lesbian detective/ disappearing homophobes/upper class gay society. ISBN 0-941483-25-8 8.95

THE FINER GRAIN by Denise Ohio. 216 pp. Brilliant young college lesbian novel. ISBN 0-941483-11-8 8.95

THE AMAZON TRAIL by Lee Lynch. 216 pp. Life, travel & lore of famous lesbian author. ISBN 0-941483-27-4 8.95

HIGH CONTRAST by Jessie Lattimore. 264 pp. Women of the Crystal Palace. ISBN 0-941483-17-7 8.95

OCTOBER OBSESSION by Meredith More. Josie's rich, secret Lesbian life. ISBN 0-941483-18-5 8.95

LESBIAN CROSSROADS by Ruth Baetz. 276 pp. Contemporary Lesbian lives. ISBN 0-941483-21-5 9.95

BEFORE STONEWALL: THE MAKING OF A GAY AND LESBIAN COMMUNITY by Andrea Weiss & Greta Schiller. 96 pp., 25 illus. ISBN 0-941483-20-7 7.95

WE WALK THE BACK OF THE TIGER by Patricia A. Murphy. 192 pp. Romantic Lesbian novel/beginning women's movement. ISBN 0-941483-13-4 8.95

SUNDAY'S CHILD by Joyce Bright. 216 pp. Lesbian athletics, at last the novel about sports. ISBN 0-941483-12-6 8.95

OSTEN'S BAY by Zenobia N. Vole. 204 pp. Sizzling adventure romance set on Bonaire. ISBN 0-941483-15-0 8.95

LESSONS IN MURDER by Claire McNab. 216 pp. 1st Det. Inspec. Carol Ashton mystery — erotic tension!. ISBN 0-941483-14-2 8.95

YELLOWTHROAT by Penny Hayes. 240 pp. Margarita, bandit, kidnaps Julia. ISBN 0-941483-10-X 8.95

SAPPHISTRY: THE BOOK OF LESBIAN SEXUALITY by Pat Califia. 3d edition, revised. 208 pp. ISBN 0-941483-24-X 8.95

CHERISHED LOVE by Evelyn Kennedy. 192 pp. Erotic Lesbian love story. ISBN 0-941483-08-8 8.95

LAST SEPTEMBER by Helen R. Hull. 208 pp. Six stories & a glorious novella. ISBN 0-941483-09-6 8.95

THE SECRET IN THE BIRD by Camarin Grae. 312 pp. Striking, psychological suspense novel. ISBN 0-941483-05-3 8.95

TO THE LIGHTNING by Catherine Ennis. 208 pp. Romantic Lesbian 'Robinson Crusoe' adventure. ISBN 0-941483-06-1 8.95

THE OTHER SIDE OF VENUS by Shirley Verel. 224 pp. Luminous, romantic love story. ISBN 0-941483-07-X 8.95

DREAMS AND SWORDS by Katherine V. Forrest. 192 pp. Romantic, erotic, imaginative stories. ISBN 0-941483-03-7 8.95

MEMORY BOARD by Jane Rule. 336 pp. Memorable novel about an aging Lesbian couple. ISBN 0-941483-02-9 9.95

THE ALWAYS ANONYMOUS BEAST by Lauren Wright Douglas. 224 pp. A Caitlin Reece mystery. First in a series. ISBN 0-941483-04-5 8.95

SEARCHING FOR SPRING by Patricia A. Murphy. 224 pp. Novel about the recovery of love. ISBN 0-941483-00-2 8.95

DUSTY'S QUEEN OF HEARTS DINER by Lee Lynch. 240 pp. Romantic blue-collar novel. ISBN 0-941483-01-0 8.95

PARENTS MATTER by Ann Muller. 240 pp. Parents' relationships with Lesbian daughters and gay sons. ISBN 0-930044-91-6 9.95

THE PEARLS by Shelley Smith. 176 pp. Passion and fun in the Caribbean sun. ISBN 0-930044-93-2 7.95

MAGDALENA by Sarah Aldridge. 352 pp. Epic Lesbian novel set on three continents. ISBN 0-930044-99-1 8.95

THE BLACK AND WHITE OF IT by Ann Allen Shockley. 144 pp. Short stories. ISBN 0-930044-96-7 7.95

SAY JESUS AND COME TO ME by Ann Allen Shockley. 288 pp. Contemporary romance. ISBN 0-930044-98-3 8.95

LOVING HER by Ann Allen Shockley. 192 pp. Romantic love story. ISBN 0-930044-97-5 7.95

MURDER AT THE NIGHTWOOD BAR by Katherine V. Forrest. 240 pp. A Kate Delafield mystery. Second in a series. ISBN 0-930044-92-4 8.95

ZOE'S BOOK by Gail Pass. 224 pp. Passionate, obsessive love story. ISBN 0-930044-95-9 7.95

WINGED DANCER by Camarin Grae. 228 pp. Erotic Lesbian adventure story. ISBN 0-930044-88-6 8.95

PAZ by Camarin Grae. 336 pp. Romantic Lesbian adventurer with the power to change the world. ISBN 0-930044-89-4 8.95

SOUL SNATCHER by Camarin Grae. 224 pp. A puzzle, an adventure, a mystery — Lesbian romance. ISBN 0-930044-90-8 8.95

THE LOVE OF GOOD WOMEN by Isabel Miller. 224 pp. Long-awaited new novel by the author of the beloved *Patience and Sarah.* ISBN 0-930044-81-9 8.95

THE HOUSE AT PELHAM FALLS by Brenda Weathers. 240 pp. Suspenseful Lesbian ghost story. ISBN 0-930044-79-7 7.95

HOME IN YOUR HANDS by Lee Lynch. 240 pp. More stories from the author of *Old Dyke Tales.* ISBN 0-930044-80-0 7.95

EACH HAND A MAP by Anita Skeen. 112 pp. Real-life poems that touch us all. ISBN 0-930044-82-7 6.95

SURPLUS by Sylvia Stevenson. 342 pp. A classic early Lesbian novel. ISBN 0-930044-78-9 7.95

PEMBROKE PARK by Michelle Martin. 256 pp. Derring-do and daring romance in Regency England. ISBN 0-930044-77-0 7.95

THE LONG TRAIL by Penny Hayes. 248 pp. Vivid adventures of two women in love in the old west. ISBN 0-930044-76-2 8.95

HORIZON OF THE HEART by Shelley Smith. 192 pp. Hot romance in summertime New England. ISBN 0-930044-75-4 7.95

AN EMERGENCE OF GREEN by Katherine V. Forrest. 288 pp. Powerful novel of sexual discovery. ISBN 0-930044-69-X 9.95

THE LESBIAN PERIODICALS INDEX edited by Claire Potter. 432 pp. Author & subject index. ISBN 0-930044-74-6 29.95

DESERT OF THE HEART by Jane Rule. 224 pp. A classic; basis for the movie *Desert Hearts.* ISBN 0-930044-73-8 8.95

SPRING FORWARD/FALL BACK by Sheila Ortiz Taylor. 288 pp. Literary novel of timeless love. ISBN 0-930044-70-3 7.95

FOR KEEPS by Elisabeth Nonas. 144 pp. Contemporary novel about losing and finding love. ISBN 0-930044-71-1 7.95

TORCHLIGHT TO VALHALLA by Gale Wilhelm. 128 pp. Classic novel by a great Lesbian writer. ISBN 0-930044-68-1 7.95